Deltora Quest

CITY OF THE RATS

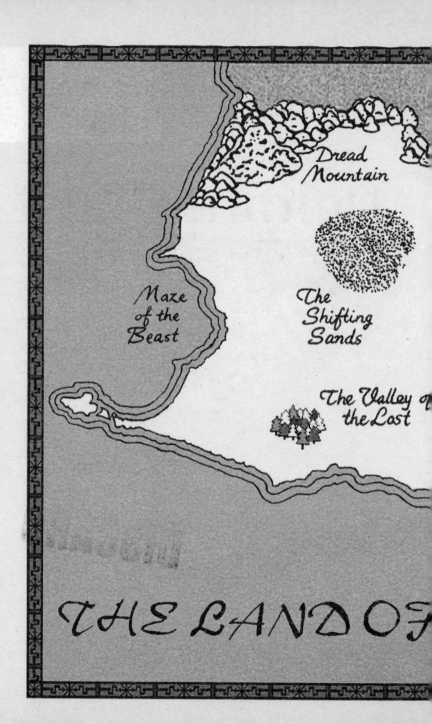

The Shadowlands

The Lake
of Tears

City
of the
Rats

The Forests
of Silence

Del

N
W E
S

DELTORA

VENTURE INTO DELTORA

Deltora Quest

CITY OF THE RATS

EMILY RODDA

Scholastic Inc.

New York   Toronto   London   Auckland
Sydney   Mexico City   New Delhi   Hong Kong

No part of this publication may be reproduced, stored in a retrieval system, or transmitted in any form or by any means, electronic, mechanical, photocopying, recording, or otherwise, without written permission of the publisher. For information regarding permission, write to Permissions Department, Scholastic Australia, PO Box 579, Lindfield, New South Wales, Australia 2070.

ISBN 978-0-545-46022-4

Text and graphics copyright © 2000 by Emily Rodda
Deltora Quest concept and characters copyright © Emily Rodda
Deltora Quest is a registered trademark of Rin Pty Ltd.
Cover illustrations copyright © 2000 by Scholastic Australia
Cover illustrations by Marc McBride
Graphics by Kate Rowe
Cover design by Natalie Sousa
First published by Scholastic Australia Pty Limited

All rights reserved. Published by Scholastic Inc., 557 Broadway, New York, NY 10012, by arrangement with Scholastic Press, an imprint of Scholastic Australia.

SCHOLASTIC and associated logos are trademarks and/or registered trademarks of Scholastic Inc.

12 11 10 9 8 7 6 5 4 3 2 1   12 13 14 15 16 17/0

Printed in the U.S.A.   40
This edition first printing, June 2012

Contents

The story so far . . .

Sixteen-year-old Lief, fulfilling a pledge made by his father before he was born, has set out on a great quest to find the seven gems of the magic Belt of Deltora. The Belt is all that can save the kingdom from the tyranny of the evil Shadow Lord, who, only months before Lief's birth, invaded Deltora and enslaved its people with the help of sorcery and his fearsome Grey Guards.

The gems — an amethyst, a topaz, a diamond, a ruby, an opal, a lapis lazuli, and an emerald — were stolen to open the way for the evil Shadow Lord to invade the kingdom. Now they lie hidden in dark and terrible places throughout the land. Only when they have been restored to the Belt can the heir to Deltora's throne be found, and the Shadow Lord defeated.

Lief's companions are the man Barda, who was once a Palace guard, and Jasmine, a wild, orphaned girl of Lief's own age who they met in the fearful Forests of Silence.

In the Forests they discovered the amazing healing powers of the nectar of the Lilies of Life. There they also won the first gem — the golden topaz, symbol of faith, which has the power to bring the living into contact with the spirit world, and to clear and sharpen the mind. At the Lake of Tears, they broke the evil enchantment of the sorceress Thaegan, released the peoples of Raladin and D'Or from her curse, and won the second gem — the great ruby, symbol of happiness, which pales when misfortune threatens its wearer.

Now read on . . .

1 - The Trap

Footsore and weary, Lief, Barda, and Jasmine moved west, towards the fabled City of the Rats. They knew little about their goal except that it was a place of evil, deserted by its people long ago. But they were almost sure that one of the seven lost gems of the Belt of Deltora lay hidden there.

They had been walking steadily all day and now, as the glowing sun slipped towards the horizon, they longed to stop for rest. But the road on which they walked, deeply rutted with the tracks of wagons, threaded through a plain where thornbushes had taken hold and spread, covering the land. The thorns lined the road without break, and extended as far as the eye could see.

Lief sighed, and for comfort touched the Belt hidden under his shirt. It held two gems now: the golden topaz and the scarlet ruby. Both had been won against great odds, and in the process of winning them, great things had been done.

The people of Raladin, with whom they had stayed for the last two weeks, did not know of their quest to find the lost gems. Manus, the Ralad man who had shared the search for the ruby, was sworn to silence. But it was no secret that the companions had caused the death of the evil sorceress Thaegan, ally of the evil Shadow Lord. It was no secret, either, that two of Thaegan's thirteen children had gone the way of their mother. The Ralads, freed at last from Thaegan's curse, had made many songs of joy, praising the companions for their deeds.

It had been hard to leave them. Hard to leave Manus, and the happiness, safety, good food, and warm, soft beds of the hidden village. But five gems were still to be found, and until they were restored to the Belt, the Shadow Lord's tyranny over Deltora could not be broken. The three companions had to move on.

"These thorns are never-ending," Jasmine complained, her voice breaking into Lief's thoughts. He turned to look at her. As usual, the little furred creature called Filli was nestled on her shoulder, blinking through Jasmine's mass of black hair. Kree, the raven, who was never far out of her sight, was swooping over the thorns nearby, catching insects. He, at least, was filling his belly.

"There is something ahead!" called Barda. He

pointed to a glimmer of white on the side of the road.

Curious and hopeful, they hurried to the place. There, sticking out of the thorns, was a strange signpost.

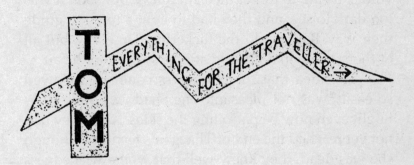

"What does it mean?" Jasmine murmured.

"It seems to point the way to some sort of shop," said Lief.

"What is a shop?"

Lief glanced at the girl in surprise, then remembered that she had spent her life in the Forests of Silence, and had never seen many of the things he took for granted.

"A shop is a place for buying and selling goods," Barda explained. "In the city of Del, these days, the shops are poor, and many are closed. But once, before the Shadow Lord, there were many, selling food and drink and clothes and other things to the people."

Jasmine looked at him with her head to one side. Lief realized that even now she did not understand. For her, food grew on trees and drink ran in the streams. Other things were found or made — and what you could not find or make, you did without.

They tramped on up the road, talking in low voices, trying to forget their tiredness. But soon it was too dark to see, and they had to light a torch to guide their way. Barda held the flickering flame low, but all of them knew that it could still be seen from the air.

The idea that their progress could be followed so easily was not pleasant. The Shadow Lord's spies might even now be patrolling the skies. Also, they had not yet reached the end of Thaegan's territory. Though she was dead, they knew well that where wickedness had held sway for so long, danger threatened everywhere.

About an hour after they had lit the torch, Jasmine stopped, and glanced behind her. "We are being followed," she breathed. "Not just by one, but by many."

Though they themselves could hear nothing, Lief and Barda did not bother asking her how she knew. They had learned that Jasmine's senses were far keener and sharper than their own. She might not know what shops were, she might not be able to read and write more than a little, but in other ways her knowledge was vast.

"They know we are ahead," she whispered. "They stop when we stop, and move when we move."

Silently Lief pulled up his shirt and looked down at the ruby in the Belt around his waist. His heart thudded as he saw, by the flickering light of the torch, that the deep red gem had faded to a dull pink.

Barda and Jasmine were looking at the stone also. They knew, as Lief did, that the ruby paled when danger threatened its wearer. Its message, now, was clear.

"So," Barda muttered. "Our followers have evil intent. Who are they? Could Kree fly back, and — ?"

"Kree is not an owl!" snapped Jasmine. "He cannot see in the dark, any more than we can." She crouched, put her ear to the ground, and frowned, listening intently. "The followers are not Grey Guards, at least," she said at last. "They move too quietly for that, and they are not marching in time."

"It is a band of robbers, perhaps, thinking to ambush us when we stop to sleep or rest. We must turn and fight!" Lief's hand was already on the hilt of his sword. The songs of the Ralad people were ringing in his ears. What was a ragged crew of robbers compared to the monsters he, Barda, and Jasmine had faced and defeated?

"The middle of a road hemmed in by thorns is no good place to make a stand, Lief," said Barda grimly. "And there is nowhere here that we could hide, to take enemies by surprise. We should move on, to try to find a better place."

5

They began to walk again, faster now. Lief kept glancing behind him, but there was nothing to be seen in the shadows at his back.

They came to a dead tree that stood like a ghost at the side of the road, its white trunk rising out of the thornbushes. Moments after they had passed it, Lief sensed a change in the air. The back of his neck began to prickle.

"They are gaining speed," Jasmine panted.

Then they heard it. A long, low howl that chilled the blood.

Filli, clutching Jasmine's shoulder, made a small, frightened sound. Lief saw that the fur was standing up all over his tiny body.

There was another howl, and another.

"Wolves!" hissed Jasmine. "We cannot outrun them. They are almost upon us!"

She tore two more torches from her pack and thrust them into the flame of the one she already held. "They will fear the fire," she said, pushing the newly burning sticks into Lief's and Barda's hands. "But we must face them. We must not turn our backs."

"We are to walk backwards all the way to Tom's shop?" Lief joked feebly, gripping his torch. But Jasmine did not smile, and neither did Barda. He was staring back at the dead tree glimmering white in the distance.

"They did not make their move until we were past that tree," he muttered. "They wished to prevent us climbing it, and escaping them. These are no ordinary wolves."

"Be ready," Jasmine warned.

She already had her dagger in her hand. Lief and Barda drew their swords. They stood together, the torches held high, waiting.

And with another chorus of bloodcurdling howls, out of the darkness surged what seemed a sea of moving pinpoints of yellow light — the eyes of the wolves.

Jasmine lashed her torch from side to side in front of her. Lief and Barda did the same, so that the road in front of them was blocked by a moving line of flame.

The beasts slowed, but still moved forward, growling. As they came closer to the light, Lief could see that, indeed, they were no ordinary wolves. They were huge, covered with shaggy, matted fur striped with brown and yellow. Their lips curled back from their snarling jaws and their open, dripping mouths were not red inside, but black.

He counted them quickly. There were eleven. For some reason, that number meant something to him, but he could not think why. In any case, there was no time to worry about such things. With Barda and Jasmine he began to back away, keeping his torch moving. But for every step the companions took, the beasts took one, too.

Lief remembered his weak joke. 'We are to walk

backwards all the way to Tom's shop?" he had asked.

Now it looked as though they might be forced to do just that. The beasts are driving us, he thought.

The beasts are driving us . . . They are not ordinary wolves . . . There are eleven . . .

His stomach lurched. "Barda! Jasmine!" he hissed. "These are not wolves. They are . . ."

But he never finished. For at that moment he and his companions took another step back, the great net trap that had been set for them was sprung, and they were swung, shrieking, into the air.

2 - Roast Meat

Crushed together in the net, bundled so tightly that they could hardly move, Lief, Barda, and Jasmine swung sickeningly in midair. They were helpless. Their torches and weapons had flown from their hands as they were whipped off their feet. Kree swooped around them, screeching in despair.

The net was hanging from a tree growing by the side of the track. Unlike the other tree they had seen, it was alive. The branch that supported the net was thick and strong — too strong to break.

Below, wolf howls were changing to bellows of triumph. Lief looked down. In the light of the fallen torches he could see that the beasts' bodies were bulging, transforming into humanlike forms.

In moments, eleven hideous, grinning creatures were capering on the track below the tree. Some were large, some were small. Some were covered in hair, others were completely bald. They were green, brown, yellow, sickly white — even slimy red. One had six stumpy legs. But Lief knew who they were.

They were the sorceress Thaegan's children. He remembered the rhyme that listed their names.

Hot, Tot, Jin, Jod,
Fie, Fly, Zan, Zod,
Pik, Snik, Lun, Lod,
And the dreaded Ichabod.

Jin and Jod were dead — smothered in their own quicksand trap. Now only eleven of the thirteen remained. But they were all here. They had gathered together to hunt the enemies who had caused the deaths of their mother, brother, and sister. They wanted revenge.

Grunting and snuffling, some of the monsters were tearing thornbushes up by the roots and piling them beneath the swinging net. Others were picking up the torches and dancing around, chanting:

More heat, more heat,
Tender, juicy roast meat!
Watch the fun,
Till it's done.
Hear its groans,
Crack its bones!
More heat, more heat,
Tender, juicy roast meat!

"They are going to burn us!" groaned Barda,

struggling vainly. "Jasmine, your second dagger. Can you reach it?"

"Do you think that I would still be hanging here if I could?" Jasmine whispered back furiously.

The monsters below were cheering as they threw the torches onto the pile of thorns. Already Lief could feel warmth below him, and smell smoke. He knew that soon the green bushes would dry and catch alight. Then he and his friends would roast in the heat, and when the net burned through they would fall into the fire.

Something soft moved against Lief's cheek. It was Filli. The little creature had managed to work his way off Jasmine's shoulder and now was squeezing through the net right beside Lief's ear.

He, at least, was free. But he did not run up the ropes and into the tree above, as Lief expected. Instead, he remained clinging to the net, nibbling at it desperately. Lief realized that he was going to try to make a hole big enough for them to climb through.

It was a brave effort, but how much time would it take for those tiny teeth to gnaw through such thick, strong netting? Too much time. Long before Filli had made even a small gap, the monsters below would notice what he was doing. Then they would drive him away, or kill him.

There was a howl of rage from the ground. Lief looked down in panic. Had their enemies caught sight of Filli already? No — they were not looking up. Instead, they were glaring at one another.

"Two legs for Ichabod!" the biggest one was roaring, beating his lumpy red chest. "Two legs *and* a head."

"No! No!" two green creatures snarled, baring dripping brown teeth. "Not fair! Fie and Fly say no!"

"They are fighting over which parts of us they will eat!" exclaimed Barda. "Can you believe it?"

"Let them fight," muttered Jasmine. "The more they fight, the more time Filli has to do his work."

"We share the meat!" shrieked the two smallest monsters, their piercing voices rising above the noise of the others. "Hot and Tot say equal shares."

Their brothers and sisters growled and muttered.

"Are they not stupid?" Lief shouted suddenly, pretending that he was talking to Barda and Jasmine. "Do they not know that they cannot have equal shares!"

"Lief, are you mad?" hissed Jasmine.

But Lief went on shouting. He could see that the monsters had grown still, and were listening. "There are three of us, and eleven of them!" he roared. "You cannot divide three fairly into eleven parts. It is impossible!"

He knew as well as Jasmine did that he was taking a risk. The monsters could look up at him, and see Filli at the same time. But he was gambling on the hope that suspicion and anger would make them keep their eyes fixed on one another.

And, to his relief, he saw that his gamble had succeeded. The monsters had begun muttering together in small groups, glancing slyly at one another.

"If they were nine only, they could cut each of us into three parts and have one part each," he shouted. "But as it is . . ."

"Equal shares!" shrieked Hot and Tot. "Hot and Tot say — "

Ichabod pounced upon them and knocked their heads together with a sharp crack. They fell senseless to the ground.

"Now," he snarled. "Now there be equal shares, like you want. Now we be nine."

The fire had begun to blaze and crackle. Smoke billowed upwards, making Lief cough. He looked sideways and saw that Filli had already succeeded in making a small hole in the net. Now he was working on enlarging it. But he needed more time.

"There is something they have forgotten, Lief," Barda said loudly. "If we are each divided into three, the shares will still not be equal. Why, I am twice the size of Jasmine! Whoever gets a third part of her will not do well at all. Really, she should be divided in half!"

"Yes," agreed Lief, just as loudly, ignoring Jasmine's cries of rage. "But that would only make eight pieces, Barda. And there are nine to feed!"

He watched out of the corner of his eye as Zan, the six-legged monster, nodded thoughtfully, then swung around and clubbed his neighbor, who happened to be Fie, felling her to the ground.

Fly, furious at the attack on his twin, leaped onto Zan's back, screeching and biting. Zan roared, lurched around, and knocked over the hairy brother on his other side, who in turn fell over the sister in front of him, stabbing himself on her horns.

And then, suddenly, they were all fighting — shrieking, biting, and bashing — crashing into the thornbushes, tumbling into the fire, rolling on the ground.

The fight went on, and on. And by the time Filli had finished his work, and the three companions had escaped from the net and climbed into the tree above, there was only one monster left standing. Ichabod.

Surrounded by the bodies of his fallen brothers and sisters, he stood by the fire, bellowing and beating his chest in triumph. Any moment he would look up and see that the net was empty, and that the food he had fought for was in the tree — with nowhere to go.

"We must take him by surprise," whispered Jasmine, pulling her second dagger from her leggings and checking that Filli was safely on her shoulder again. "It is the only way."

Without another word, she jumped, striking Ichabod on the back with both feet. Knocked off balance, he fell into the fire, landing with a crash and a roar.

14

Gathering their wits, Barda and Lief slid down the tree as quickly as they could and ran to where Jasmine was snatching up her dagger and their swords.

"Why did you wait?" she demanded, thrusting their swords at them. "Make haste!"

With Kree soaring above, they ran like the wind along the track, careless of the ruts in the road and the darkness. Behind them, Ichabod was howling in rage and pain as he crawled from the fire and began stumbling after them.

3 - Everything for the Traveller

Panting, chests aching, ears straining for the sound of howls behind them, they ran on. They all knew that if Ichabod changed into a wolf or other beast, he could catch them easily. But they heard nothing.

It is possible that he cannot transform when he is injured, thought Lief. If so, we are safe. But, like his companions, he did not dare to stop or slow.

Finally they came to a place where the track crossed a shallow stream.

"I am sure that this marks the border of Thaegan's lands," gasped Barda. "See? There are no thornbushes on the other side. Ichabod will not follow us across."

Legs trembling with weariness, they splashed through the cold water. On the other side of the stream the track continued, but soft, green grass and small trees grew beside it, and they could see the shapes of wildflowers.

They staggered on for a little, then turned from the track and fell down in the shelter of a grove of the small trees. Leaves whispering overhead, grass soft under their heads, they slept.

✳

When they woke, the sun was high, and Kree was calling them. Lief stretched and yawned. His muscles were stiff and aching after the long run, and his feet were sore.

"We should have slept in turns," Barda groaned, sitting up and easing his back. "It was dangerous to trust in our safety, so close to the border."

"We were all tired. And Kree was watching." Jasmine had jumped up, and was already prowling around the grove. She felt no stiffness, it seemed.

She put her hand to the rough trunk of one of the trees. Above her, leaves stirred faintly. She put her head to one side, and seemed to listen.

"The trees say that carts still use this road quite often," she announced finally. "Heavy carts, drawn by horses. But there is nothing ahead today."

Before starting off again, they ate a little of the bread, honey, and fruit that the Ralads had given them. Filli had his share, as well as a piece of honeycomb, his favorite treat.

Then they moved on slowly. After a time, they saw another of the signs directing them to Tom's shop.

"I hope Tom sells something for sore feet," muttered Lief.

"The sign says, 'Everything for the Traveller,' " Barda said. "So no doubt he does. But we must choose only what we really need. We have little money."

Jasmine glanced at them. She said nothing, but Lief noticed that she began to walk a little faster. Plainly, she was curious to see exactly what a shop was like.

An hour later they rounded a bend and saw, sticking up from the middle of a grove of trees, a long, jagged metal shape, like a lightning bolt. Huge metal letters stuck out from the side of the shape.

Wondering, they walked on. As they moved closer to the place they saw that the trees were in the shape of a horseshoe, clustering around the sides and back of a strange little stone building. The jagged shape supporting the metal letters plunged right into the middle of its peaked roof, as though the building were being struck by lightning.

Plainly, this was Tom's shop, though at first glance it looked rather more like an inn than a place where things could be bought. There was a flat, cleared space between the building and the road — space enough for several carts to stop — and here and there stood great stone troughs filled with water for animals to drink. But a large shop window shone on one side of the door, and on the glass the shop owner's name had been painted in bright red letters — arranged from top to bottom, like they were on the chimney sign and the signposts the travellers had passed.

"This Tom certainly likes to let people know his name." Barda grinned. "Very well, then. Let us see what he has for us."

They crossed the cleared space and peered into the shop window. It was filled with packs, hats, belts, boots, socks, waterbags, coats, ropes, pots and pans, and many, many other things, including some that Lief did not recognize. Strangely, there were no prices or labels, but right in the middle was a yellow sign.

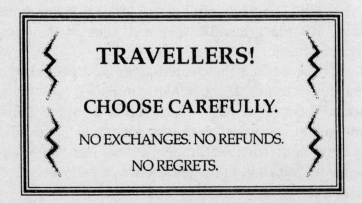

A bell fastened to the door tinkled as they entered the shop, but no one came forward to greet them. They looked around, blinking in the gloom. The crowded room seemed very dim after the bright sunlight outside. Narrow corridors ran between shelves that rose from the floor to the low ceiling. The shelves were crammed with goods. At the far end was a dusty counter cluttered with account books, a set of scales, and what looked like a money tin. Behind the counter were more shelves, a door, and another sign:

TRAVELLERS!

CHOOSE CAREFULLY.

NO EXCHANGES. NO REFUNDS.

NO REGRETS.

"Tom is a trusting fellow," Barda said, looking around. "Why, we could have come in here, stolen whatever we liked, and walked out again, by now."

To prove his point, he reached for a small lantern on the shelf closest to him. When he tried to pick it up, however, the lantern would not move.

Barda's jaw dropped in astonishment. He tugged, but without success. Finally, as Lief doubled up with laughter and Jasmine stared, he gave up. But when he tried to take his hand away from the lantern, he could not. He heaved, cursing, but his fingers were stuck fast.

"You want a lantern, friend?"

They all jumped violently and spun around. A tall, lean man with a hat on the back of his head was standing behind the counter, his arms folded and his wide mouth curved in a mocking smile.

"What *is* this?" shouted Barda angrily, jabbing his free hand at the lantern.

"It is proof that Tom is *not* a trusting fellow," the man behind the counter said, his smile broadening. He put a long finger below the counter, and perhaps he pressed a button there, because suddenly Barda's hand was released. He jerked backwards, bumping into Lief and Jasmine with some force.

"Now," said the man behind the counter. "What can Tom show you? And more to the point, what can Tom *sell* you?" He rubbed his hands.

"We need a good length of strong rope," said

Lief, seeing that Barda was going to say nothing. "And also, something for sore feet, if you have it."

"Have it?" cried Tom. "Of course I have it. Everything for the traveller. Did you not see the sign?"

He eased himself out from behind the counter and selected a coil of thin rope from a shelf.

"This is my very best," he said. "Light, and very strong. Three silver coins, and it is yours."

"Three silver coins for a piece of rope?" Barda exploded. "That is robbery!"

Tom's smile did not waver. "Not robbery, friend, but business," he said calmly. "For where else will you find a rope like this?"

Holding one end of the rope, he threw the rest upwards with a flick of his wrist. The rope uncoiled like a snake and wound itself tightly around one of the ceiling rafters. Tom pulled at it, to show its strength. Then he flicked his wrist again, and the rope unwrapped itself from the rafter and dropped back into his hands, winding itself up into a neat coil as it fell.

"Trickery," growled Barda, glowering.

But Lief was fascinated. "We will take it," he said excitedly, ignoring Barda's elbow in his ribs, and Jasmine's suspicious frown.

Tom rubbed his hands. "I knew you were a man who understood a bargain," he said. "Now. What else might I show you? No obligation to buy!"

Lief looked around excitedly. If this shop had

rope that acted as though it were alive, what other wonders might it hold?

"Everything!" he exclaimed. "We want to see everything!"

Tom beamed.

Jasmine moved uncomfortably. It was clear that she did not like the crowded shop, with its low ceiling, and she did not much like Tom, either. "Filli and I will wait outside with Kree," she announced. She turned on her heel and left.

The next hour flew by as Tom showed Lief cushioned socks for sore feet, telescopes that saw around corners, plates that cleaned themselves, and pipes that blew bubbles of light. He showed machines to predict the weather, little white circles that looked like paper but swelled up to full-size loaves of bread when water was added, an axe that never blunted, a bedroll that floated off the ground, tiny beads that made fire, and a hundred more amazing inventions.

Slowly, Barda forgot his suspicion and began to watch, ask questions, and join in. By the time Tom had finished, he was quite won over, and as eager as Lief was to have as many of these marvels as they could afford. There were such wonderful things . . . things that would make their travels easier, safer, and more comfortable.

At last, Tom folded his arms and stood back, smiling at them. "So," he said. "Tom has shown you. Now, what can he sell you?"

4 - Money Matters

Some of Tom's goods, like the floating bedroll, cost more by themselves than all the money Lief and Barda had. But other things they could afford, and it was difficult to decide between them.

In the end, as well as the self-coiling rope, they chose a packet of "No Bakes" — the white rounds that expanded into loaves of bread — a jar of "Pure and Clear" — a powder that made any water fit to drink — and some cushioned socks. The pile was disappointingly small, and they had had to put aside many far more interesting things, including a jar of the fire-making beads and the pipe that blew bubbles of light.

"If only we had more money!" Lief exclaimed.

"Ah!" said Tom, pushing his hat a little back on his head. "Well, perhaps we can make a bargain. I buy as well as sell." He cast a sly glance at Lief's sword.

But Lief shook his head firmly. Much as he

24

wanted Tom's goods, he would not give up the sword his father had made for him on their own forge.

Tom shrugged. "Your cloak is a little stained," he said casually. "But still, I could perhaps give you something for it."

This time Lief smiled. However uncaring Tom appeared to be, he plainly knew very well that the cloak Lief's mother had woven for him had special powers.

"This cloak can make its wearer almost invisible," he said. "It has saved our lives more than once. I fear it is not for sale either."

Tom sighed. "A pity," he said. "Ah, well." He began to pack the fire beads and the light pipe away.

At that moment the bell on the shop door tinkled, and a stranger walked in. He was as tall as Barda, and as powerful, with long, tangled black hair and a shaggy black beard. A jagged scar ran down one cheek, showing pale against his brown skin.

Lief saw Jasmine slipping inside after him. She stood against the door, her hand on the dagger at her belt. Clearly, she was ready for trouble.

The stranger nodded briefly to Lief and Barda, snatched up a length of the self-coiling rope from a shelf, and strode past them to lean over the dusty counter.

"How much?" he asked Tom abruptly.

"One silver coin to you, good sir," said Tom.

Lief's eyes widened. Tom had told them that the

price of the rope was *three* silver coins. He opened his mouth to protest, then felt Barda's warning hand on his wrist. He glanced up and saw that his companion's eyes were fixed on the counter, near to where the stranger's hands were resting. There was a mark there. The stranger had drawn it in the dust.

The secret sign of resistance to the Shadow Lord! The sign that they had seen scratched on walls so many times on their way to the Lake of Tears! By drawing it on the counter, the stranger had signalled to Tom. And Tom had responded by lowering the price of the rope.

The man threw a silver coin into Tom's hand and as he did his sleeve casually wiped the mark away. It all happened very quickly. If Lief had not seen the mark with his own eyes, he would not have believed it was ever there.

"I have heard rumors of strange happenings at the Lake of Tears, and indeed all through the territory across the stream," the stranger said carelessly, as he turned to go. "I have heard that Thaegan is no more."

"Indeed?" said Tom smoothly. "I cannot tell you. I am but a poor shopkeeper, and know nothing of these things. The thorns by the road, I understand, are as wild as ever."

The other man snorted. "The thorns are not the result of sorcery, but of a hundred years of poverty and neglect. The Del King's thorns, I call them, as do many others."

Lief's heart sank. By making the secret sign, this stranger had proved that he was dedicated to resisting the Shadow Lord. But plainly he hated the memory of the kings and queens of Deltora as much as Lief himself had once done, and blamed them for the kingdom's misfortune.

He knew he could say nothing, but could not help staring at the man as he passed. The man returned his gaze, unsmiling, and left the shop, brushing past Jasmine as he went through the door.

"Who was that?" Barda whispered to Tom.

The shopkeeper settled his hat on his head more firmly before replying. "No names are mentioned in Tom's shop but Tom's own, sir," he said calmly. "It is better so, in these hard times."

Lief heard the door tinkle again and turned to see Jasmine leaving. Now that the possibility of danger had passed, she had become restless, and had decided to go out into the fresh air once more.

Perhaps Tom realized that Barda and Lief had

seen and understood the mark the stranger had made on the counter, for suddenly he picked up the fire beads and the light pipe, and added them to their little pile of goods.

"No extra charge," he said, as they glanced at him in surprise. "Tom is always happy to help a traveller — as you have seen."

"A traveller who is on the right side." Barda smiled.

But Tom merely raised his eyebrows, as if he had no idea what the big man meant, and held out his hand for payment.

"A pleasure to serve you, sirs," he said, as they handed over their money. He counted the coins rapidly, nodded, and put them away in his cash box.

"And what of our free gift?" asked Lief cheekily. "The sign in the window says — "

"Ah, of course," said Tom. "The gift." He bent and fumbled under the counter. When he stood up, he was holding a small, flat tin box. He handed it to Lief.

"If you do not ask, you do not get. Is that your motto, young sir?" he asked. "Well, it is my motto too."

Lief looked at the box. It fitted easily into the palm of his hand, and looked quite old. The faded lettering on the label said simply:

"What is it?" Lief asked, bewildered.

"The instructions are on the back," said Tom.

Suddenly, he paused, listening. Then he slipped out from behind the counter and darted through the shop's back door.

In his haste he had left the door open, and Lief and Barda followed him. To their surprise, the door led directly into a small field enclosed by a white fence and completely hidden from the road by the tall trees that surrounded it. Three grey horses were standing by the fence, and sitting upon it, patting them, was Jasmine, with Kree perched on her shoulder.

Tom strode towards the fence, waving his arms. "Do not touch the animals, if you please!" he shouted. "They are valuable."

"I am not hurting them!" exclaimed Jasmine indignantly, but she took her hand away. The beasts snuffled in disappointment.

"Horses!" Barda muttered to Lief. "If only we

had horses to ride! How much faster would our journey be then?"

Lief nodded slowly. He had never ridden before, and he was sure that Jasmine had not, either. But surely they could soon learn. On horseback they would be able to outrun any enemy — even Grey Guards.

"Will you sell us the beasts?" he asked, as they caught up with Tom. "For example, if we were to return to you all the things we have bought, would that be enough — ?"

Tom looked at him sharply. "No exchanges!" he snapped. "No refunds! No regrets!"

Lief's stomach lurched with disappointment.

"What are you talking about?" demanded Jasmine. "What is this 'buy' and 'sell'?"

Tom stared at her in surprise. "Your friends would like to have some beasts to ride, little miss," he explained, as though Jasmine were a small child. "But they no longer have anything to give me in exchange for them. They have spent their money on other things. And" — he glanced at Lief's cloak and sword — "they do not choose to trade anything else."

Jasmine nodded slowly, taking it in. "Perhaps, then, I have something to trade," she said. "I have many treasures."

She began to feel in her pockets, bringing out in turn a feather, a length of plaited twine, some stones, her second dagger, and the broken-toothed comb from her nest in the Forests of Silence. Tom watched her, smiling and shaking his head.

"Jasmine!" Lief called, feeling a little ashamed. "None of those things is — "

Then his jaw dropped. Barda gasped. And Tom's eyes bulged.

For Jasmine had pulled out a small bag and was carelessly upending it. Gold coins were pouring out, making a shining heap on her lap.

5 - The Bargain

Of course, Lief thought, after his first astonishment had passed. Jasmine had robbed many Grey Guards who had fallen victim to the horrors of the Forests of Silence. He had actually seen a mass of gold and silver coins among the treasures she kept in her treetop nest. But he had not realized that she had brought some of them with her when she left the Forests to join their quest. He had quite forgotten about them till now, and, because to her they were just pretty keepsakes, she had not mentioned them.

A few coins bounced away onto the ground. Barda hurried to pick them up, but Jasmine barely looked at them. She was looking at Tom — at his glittering eyes. Perhaps she did not understand about buying and selling, but she recognized greed when she saw it.

"You like this?" she asked, holding up a handful of the gold.

"Indeed I do, little miss," said Tom, recovering a little. "I like it very much."

"Then, will you exchange the horses for it?"

A strange expression crossed Tom's face — a pained expression, as though his desire for the gold was struggling with another feeling. As if he was calculating, weighing up risks.

Finally, he seemed to come to a decision.

"I cannot sell the horses," he said regretfully. "They — are promised to others. But — I have something better. If you will come this way . . ."

He led them to a shed at one side of the field. He opened the shed door and beckoned them inside.

Standing together in one corner, munching hay, were three creatures of very odd appearance. They were about the same size as horses, but had long necks, very small heads with narrow, drooping ears, and, most surprising of all, only three legs — one thick one at the front and two thinner ones at the back. They were unevenly splodged all over with black, brown, and white, as though they had been splashed with paint, and instead of hooves they had large, flat, hairy feet, each with two broad toes.

"What are they?" asked Barda, astonished.

"Why, they are muddlets," cried Tom, striding forward to turn one of the beasts towards them. "And very fine examples of the breed. Steeds fit for a king, sir. The very thing for you and your companions."

Barda, Lief, and Jasmine glanced at one another uncertainly. The idea of being able to ride instead of walk was very appealing. But the muddlets looked extremely strange.

"Their names are Noodle, Zanzee, and Pip," said Tom. Affectionately, he slapped each of the muddlets' broad rumps in turn. The beasts went on chewing hay, completely undisturbed.

"They seem gentle enough," Barda said, after a moment. "But can they run? Are they swift?"

"Swift?" exclaimed Tom, holding up his hands and rolling his eyes. "My friend, they are swift as the wind! They are strong, too — far stronger than any horse. And loyal — oh, their loyalty is famous. In addition, they eat almost anything, and thrive on hard work. Muddlets are everyone's steeds of choice, in these parts. But they are hard to get. Very hard."

"How much do you want for them?" asked Lief abruptly.

Tom rubbed his hands. "Shall we say, twenty-one gold coins for the three?" he suggested.

"Shall we say, fifteen?" growled Barda.

Tom looked shocked. "Fifteen? For these superb beasts that are as dear to me as my own children? Would you rob poor Tom? Would you make him a beggar?"

Jasmine looked concerned, but Barda's face did not quiver. "Fifteen," he repeated.

Tom threw up his hands. "Eighteen!" he said. "With saddles and bridles thrown in. Now — can I say fairer than that?"

Barda glanced at Lief and Jasmine, who both nodded vigorously.

"Very well," he said.

And so the bargain was struck. Tom fetched saddles and bridles and helped Lief, Barda, and Jasmine load the muddlets with their packs. Then he led the beasts out of the shed. They moved with a strange, rocking motion, the one front leg stepping forward first, and the two hind legs swinging together after it.

Tom opened a gate in the fence and they walked out of the field. The three grey horses watched them go. Lief felt a pang of regret. In the excitement of bargaining with Tom, he had forgotten the horses. But how nice it would have been to ride them away, instead of these other strange, lolloping creatures.

Never mind, he told himself, patting Noodle's splodgy back. We will become used to these beasts in time. By the end of our journey, no doubt, we will have grown very fond of them.

Later, he was to remember that thought — remember it bitterly.

When they reached the front of the shop, Tom held the reins while the three companions climbed up on their mounts' backs. After some discussion, Jasmine took Zanzee, Lief took Noodle, and Barda took

Pip, though in fact there was little to choose between the beasts, who looked very alike.

The saddles fitted just behind the muddlets' necks, where their bodies were narrowest. The baggage was strapped behind, across the broad expanse of the rump. It was quite a comfortable arrangement, but, all the same, Lief felt a little anxious. The ground seemed very far away, and the reins felt awkward in his hands. Suddenly he was wondering if this had been a good idea after all, though, of course, he did his best not to show it.

The muddlets were making glad, snuffling sounds. They were clearly very pleased to be out in the fresh air, and were looking forward to exercise.

"Hold the reins tightly," said Tom. "They may be a little lively at first. Call, 'Brix' when you want them to go, and 'Snuff' when you want them to stop. Call loudly, as their hearing is not sharp. Tie them up well when you stop, so they will not stray. That is all there is to it."

Lief, Barda, and Jasmine nodded.

"One more thing," Tom murmured, inspecting his fingernails. "I have not asked you where you are going, for I do not want to know. Knowledge is dangerous, in these hard times. But I am going to give you a piece of advice. It is excellent advice, and I suggest you follow it. About half an hour from here you will come to a place where the road divides. At all costs take the left path, however tempted you may be to do otherwise. Now — travel well!"

With that, he lifted a hand and slapped Noodle's rump. "Brix!" he shouted. And, with a lurching jerk, Noodle started forward, with Pip and Zanzee following close behind. Kree squawked, flapping above them.

"Remember!" Tom's voice called after them. "Keep tight reins! Be sure to take the left path!"

Lief would have liked to wave, to show that he had heard, but he did not dare lift a hand. Noodle was picking up speed, her floppy ears blowing backwards in the breeze, her powerful legs bounding forward.

Lief had never been to sea, for before he was born, the Shadow Lord had forbidden the coast to the citizens of Del. But he imagined that clinging to a lively muddlet must be very like sailing a boat in stormy weather. It required all his attention.

✳

After about ten minutes, the muddlets' excitement wore off and they slowed to a steady, lolloping pace. Noodle began to remind Lief of a rocking horse he had had as a child, rather than making him think of a pitching boat.

This is not so hard, he thought. In fact, it is easy! He was filled with pride and satisfaction. What would his friends say, if they could see him now?

The road was wide, and the companions were able to ride beside one another. Lulled by the rocking movement, Filli settled down to sleep inside Jasmine's jacket, and now that he was sure that all was well, Kree flew ahead, dipping now and then to catch an insect. Jasmine herself rode silently, her eyes thoughtful. Barda and Lief talked.

"We are making very good time," said Barda with satisfaction. "These muddlets are certainly excellent steeds. I am surprised that we have not heard of them before. I never saw one in Del."

"Tom said they were hard to get," answered Lief. "The people in this part of Deltora keep them to themselves, no doubt. And Del has had little news from the countryside since long before the Shadow Lord came."

Jasmine glanced at him, and seemed about to speak, but then she closed her mouth firmly, and said nothing. Her brows were knitted in a frown.

They rode on without speaking for a moment, and then, at last, Jasmine opened her lips.

"This place we are to go — the City of the Rats. We know nothing of it, do we?"

"Only that it is walled, appears deserted, and stands alone in the bend of a river called the Broad," said Barda. "It has been seen by travellers from afar, but I have heard not a whisper of anyone who has been inside its walls."

"Perhaps no one who has been inside has lived to tell the tale," said Jasmine grimly. "Have you considered that?"

6 ~ Noradz

Barda shrugged. "The City of the Rats has an evil reputation, and an Ak-Baba was seen in the skies above it on the morning the Shadow Lord invaded. We can be almost sure that one of the Belt's gems has been hidden there."

"So," said Jasmine, still in that hard voice, "we must go to the place, but we know little of what we will find there. We cannot prepare or plan."

"We could not prepare or plan for the Lake of Tears or the Forests of Silence," Lief put in stoutly. "But still we succeeded in both. As we will succeed in this."

Jasmine tossed her head. "Brave words!" she retorted. "Perhaps you have forgotten that in the Forests you had me to help you, and at the Lake of Tears we had Manus to guide our way. This time, it is different. We are alone, without advice or help."

Her plain speaking irritated Lief, and he could see that it irritated Barda also. Perhaps she was right in what she said, but why lower their spirits?

He turned away from her and stared straight ahead. They rode on in silence.

Shortly afterwards the road ahead of them split into two, as Tom had told them it would. There was a signpost in the middle of the fork, one arm pointing to the left, the other to the right.

"Broad River!" exclaimed Lief. "That is the river on which the City of the Rats stands! Why, what a piece of good fortune!"

Excitedly, he began turning Noodle's head to the right.

"Lief, what are you doing?" protested Jasmine. "We must take the left-hand path. Remember what the man Tom said."

"Don't you see, Jasmine? Tom would never have dreamed that we would go willingly to the City of the Rats," called Lief over his shoulder, as he urged Noodle on. "So of course he warned us against this path. But, as it happens, it is the very path we want. Come on!"

Barda and Pip were already following Lief. Still unsure, Jasmine let Zanzee carry her after them.

The track was as wide as the other, and a good, strong road, though showing the marks of cart wheels. As they moved on, the land on either side became more and more rich and green. There were no parched spaces or dead trees here. Fruits and berries grew wild everywhere, and bees hummed around the flowers, their legs weighed down by golden bags of pollen.

Far to the right there were hazy purple hills, and to the left, the green of a forest. Ahead, the road wound like a pale ribbon into the distance. The air was fresh and sweet.

The muddlets snuffled eagerly and began to pick up speed.

"They are enjoying this," laughed Lief, patting Noodle's neck.

"And so am I," called Barda in answer. "How good to ride through fertile country at last. This land, at least, has not been spoiled."

They bounded past a grove of trees and saw that not far ahead a side road branched off the main track and led away towards the purple hills. Idly, Lief wondered where it led.

Suddenly, Noodle made a strange, excited barking sound and stretched out her neck, straining against the reins. Pip and Zanzee were calling out, also. They began leaping ahead, covering great dis-

41

tances with every bound. Lief tossed and bounced on the saddle. It was taking all his strength just to hold on.

"What is the matter with them?" he shouted, as the wind beat against his face.

"I do not know!" gasped Barda. He was trying to slow Pip down, but the muddlet was taking not the slightest notice. "Snuff!" he bellowed. But Pip only ran faster, neck outstretched, mouth wide and eager.

Jasmine shrieked as Zanzee thrust his head forward, ripping the reins violently from her hands. She slipped sideways, and for a terrifying moment Lief thought she was going to fall, but she managed to throw her arms around her mount's neck, and pull herself up on the saddle once more. She clung there grimly, her head bent against the wind, as Zanzee bolted on, the stones of the road scattering under his flying feet.

There was nothing any of them could do. The muddlets were strong — far too strong for them. They thundered to the place where the side road branched, swerved off the main road in a cloud of dust, and bolted on up, up towards the hazy purple hills.

His eyes streaming, his voice hoarse from shouting, Lief saw the hills rushing towards them in a purple blur. There was something black in the midst of the purple. Lief blinked, squinted, tried to see what it was. It was coming closer, closer . . .

And then, without warning, Noodle pulled up short. Lief shot over her head, his own cry of shock ringing in his ears. Dimly he was aware of Jasmine and Barda shouting as they, too, were thrown from their mounts. Then the ground rushed up to meet him, and he knew no more.

✳

There were pains in Lief's legs and back, and his head ached. Something was nudging at his shoulder. He tried to open his eyes. At first they seemed gummed shut, but then he managed to force them open. A faceless red shape was looming over him. He tried to scream, but all that came from his throat was a strangled moan.

The red shape drew back. "This one is awake," a voice said.

A hand came down, holding a cup of water. Lief lifted his head and drank thirstily. Slowly he realized that he was lying with Barda and Jasmine on the floor of a large hall. Many torches burned around the stone walls, lighting the room and casting flickering shadows, but they did little to warm the cold air. There was a huge fireplace in one corner. It was filled with great logs, but unlit.

An overpowering smell of strong soap mingled with the smell of the burning torches. Perhaps the floor had been recently scrubbed, for the stones on which Lief lay were damp, and there was not a speck of dust anywhere.

The room was full of people. Their heads were shaved, and they were strangely dressed in close-fitting suits of black, with high boots. They were all staring intently at the companions on the floor, fascinated and fearful.

The one with the water backed away, and the towering red figure that had so frightened Lief as he returned to consciousness moved once more into his view. Now he could see that it was a man, dressed entirely in red. Even his boots were red. Gloves covered his hands, and his head was swathed in tight-fitting cloth that covered his mouth and nose, leaving a space only for the eyes. A long whip made of plaited leather hung from his wrist. It trailed behind him, swishing on the ground as he moved.

He saw that Lief had regained his senses, and was watching him. "Noradzeer," he murmured, brushing his hands down his body, from shoulders to hips. It was plainly a greeting of some kind.

Lief wanted to make sure that, whoever these strange people were, they knew he was friendly. He struggled into a sitting position and tried to copy the gesture, and the word.

The black-clad people murmured, then they too swept their hands from their shoulders to their hips and whispered, "Noradzeer, noradzeer, noradzeer . . ." till the great room was echoing with their voices.

Lief stared, his head swimming. "What — what is this place?"

"This is Noradz," said the scarlet figure, his voice muffled by the cloth that covered his mouth and nose. "Visitors are not welcome here. Why have you come?"

"We — did not mean to," Lief said. "Our mounts bolted, and carried us out of our way. We fell . . ." He winced as pain stabbed behind his eyes.

Jasmine and Barda were stirring now, and being given water in their turn. The red figure turned to them and greeted them as he had greeted Lief. Then he spoke again.

"You were lying outside our gates, with your goods scattered about you," he said, his voice cold with suspicion. "There were no mounts to be seen."

"Then they must have run away," exclaimed Jasmine impatiently. "We certainly did not throw ourselves upon the ground with such force as to knock ourselves senseless!"

The man in red drew himself up, lifting the coiling whip menacingly. "Guard your tongue, unclean one," he hissed. "Speak with respect! Do you not know that I am Reece, First Ra-Kachar of the Nine?"

Jasmine began to speak again, but Barda raised his voice, drowning her words.

"We are deeply sorry, my Lord Ra-Kachar," he

said loudly. "We are strangers, and ignorant of your ways."

"The Nine Ra-Kacharz keep the people to the holy laws of cleanliness, watchfulness, and duty," droned Reece. "Thus is the city safe. Noradzeer."

"Noradzeer," murmured the people, bending their bare heads and brushing their bodies from shoulder to thigh.

Barda and Lief glanced at each other. Both were thinking that the sooner they could leave this strange place, the happier they would be.

7 ~ Strange Customs

Jasmine was clambering to her feet, looking fretfully around the great room. The black-clad people murmured, drawing back from her as though her tattered clothing and tangled hair could somehow contaminate them.

"Where is Kree?" she demanded.

Reece turned his face towards her. "There is another of you?" he asked sharply.

"Kree is a bird," Lief explained hurriedly, as he and Barda stood up also. "A black bird."

"Kree will be waiting for you outside, Jasmine," Barda muttered under his breath. "Be still, now. Filli is safe, isn't he?"

"Yes. But he is hiding under my coat and will not come out," Jasmine hissed sullenly. "He does not like it here, and neither do I."

Barda turned to Reece and bowed. "We are most

grateful for your care of us," he said loudly. "But with your kind permission we will be on our way."

"It is our time to eat, and a platter has been prepared for you," said Reece, his dark eyes sweeping their faces as if daring them to object. "The food has already been blessed by the Nine. When food has been blessed, it must be eaten within the hour. Noradzeer."

"Noradzeer," echoed the people reverently.

Before Barda could say anything else, gongs began to sound, and two great doors at one end of the room opened to reveal a dining hall beyond. Eight tall figures, dressed in red as Reece was, stood at the opening, four on each side. The eight other Ra-Kacharz, thought Lief.

Long, leather whips hung from the Ra-Kacharz' wrists. They watched sternly as the black-clad people began shuffling past them.

Lief's head ached. He had never felt less hungry in his life. He wanted more than anything to be out of this place, but it was clear that he, Barda, and Jasmine were not to be allowed to leave until they had eaten.

Unwillingly, they walked through to the dining hall. It was as clean and scrubbed as the other room had been, and so brightly lit that every corner was visible. It was filled with bare tables, arranged in long rows. The tables were very high, with tall, slender metal legs. A plain cup and plate stood at every place, but there were no tools for eating, and no chairs. The people of Noradz, it seemed, ate with their fingers, standing up.

At the far end of the hall, a set of steps led to a raised platform. There another table stood alone. Lief guessed that this was where the Ra-Kacharz would eat, their high position giving them a good view of all that went on below.

Reece showed Lief, Barda, and Jasmine to their table, which was set a little apart from the others. Then he went to join the other Ra-Kacharz, who, as Lief had expected, were all standing at the table on the platform, facing the crowd.

When he had taken his place in the center, Reece lifted his gloved hands and surveyed the room. "Noradzeer!" he called. He swept his hands from shoulders to hips.

"Noradzeer!" echoed the people.

With one movement, all the Ra-Kacharz pulled away the cloth that swathed their mouths and noses. Immediately, gongs sounded once more, and more people in black began entering the hall, carrying huge, covered serving platters.

"I cannot think of a more uncomfortable way to eat!" Jasmine whispered. She was the smallest person in the room, and the tabletop barely reached her chin.

A serving girl came to their table and put down her burden, her hands trembling. Her light blue eyes were scared. Serving the strangers was plainly frightening for her.

"Are there no children in Noradz?" Lief asked her. "The tables are so high."

"Children eat only in the training room," the servant said in a low voice. "Children must learn the holy ways before they can grow to take their places in the hall. Noradzeer."

She removed the cover from the serving platter and Lief, Jasmine, and Barda gasped. The platter was divided into three parts. The largest held an array of tiny sausages and other meats, threaded on wooden sticks with many vegetables of every shape and color. The second was piled with golden, savory pastries and soft, white rolls. The third and smallest was filled with preserved fruits, little pink-iced cakes covered with sugar flowers, and strange-looking round, brown sweets.

Barda picked up one of the sweets and stared at it, as if amazed. "Can this be — chocolate?" he exclaimed. He popped the sweet into his mouth and closed his eyes. "It is!" he murmured blissfully. "Why, I have not tasted chocolate since I was a Palace guard! Over sixteen years!"

Lief had never seen such luxurious food in his life, and suddenly, despite everything, he felt ravenous. He picked up one of the sticks and began chewing at the meat and vegetables. The food was so delicious! Like nothing he had ever tasted before.

"This is so good!" he murmured to the serving girl, with his mouth full. She gazed at him, pleased but a little confused. Plainly, she was used to the food of Noradz, and did not know any other way of eating.

Nervously she stretched out her hand to take the heavy cover from the table. As she lifted it over the serving platter, her fingers trembled and the cover's edge caught one of the bread rolls, and knocked it from its place. The bread rolled onto the table and, before she or Lief could catch it, bounced onto the floor.

The girl screamed — a high, piercing scream of terror. At the same moment there was a cry of rage from the high table. Everyone in the room froze.

"Food is spilled!" roared the Ra-Kacharz as one. "Pick it up! Seize the offender! Seize Tira!"

Several people from the table nearest the guests spun around. One of them darted to the fallen bread and picked it up, holding it high. The others seized the serving girl. She screamed again as they began to drag her towards the high table.

Reece moved towards the steps, uncoiling his whip. "Tira spilled food upon the ground," he droned. "Spilt food is evil. Noradzeer. The evil must be driven out by one hundred strokes of the whip. Noradzeer."

"Noradzeer!" echoed the black-clad people around the tables. They watched as Tira, sobbing in fear, was cast down at Reece's feet. He raised the whip . . .

"No!" Lief darted out from his table. "Do not punish her! It was me! I did it!"

"You?" thundered Reece, lowering the whip.

"Yes!" called Lief. "I caused the food to fall. I am sorry." He knew that it was foolhardy to take the blame. But whatever the strange customs of these people, he could not bear for the girl to be punished for a simple accident.

The other Ra-Kacharz were muttering together. The one nearest Reece moved to his side and said something to him. There was a moment's stillness, broken only by the sobbing of the fallen girl. Then Reece faced Lief once more.

"You are a stranger, and unclean," he said. "You do not know our ways. The Nine have decided that you are to be spared punishment."

His voice was harsh. Clearly, he did not approve of this decision, but had been outvoted by the rest.

Breathing a sigh of relief, Lief sidled back to his table as Tira scrambled from the ground and ran, stumbling, from the room.

Barda and Jasmine greeted him with raised eyebrows. "That was a near thing," Barda muttered.

"It was a risk worth taking," Lief answered lightly, though his heart was still thudding at his near escape. "It was a fair chance that they would not punish a stranger as they would punish one of their own — at least on the first occasion."

Jasmine shrugged. She had taken vegetables from one of the sticks, and was holding them up to her shoulder, trying to coax Filli out to eat. "We should leave here as soon as we are able," she said. "These people are very strange. Who knows what other odd laws — ah, Filli, there you are!"

Tempted by the smell of the tidbits, the little creature had at last ventured to poke his nose from under the collar of Jasmine's jacket. Cautiously he crawled out onto her shoulder, took a piece of golden vegetable in his tiny paws, and began to nibble at it.

There was a sudden, strangled sound from the high table. Lief glanced up and was startled to see all the Ra-Kacharz pointing at Jasmine, their faces masks of horror.

The other people in the room turned to look. There was a moment's shocked silence. Then, suddenly, shrieking with terror, they stampeded for the doors.

"Evil!" Reece's voice thundered from the platform. "The unclean ones have brought evil to our halls. They try to destroy us! See! The creature crawls there, on her body! Kill it! Kill it!"

As one, the Nine Ra-Kacharz ran from the platform and plunged towards Jasmine, using their whips freely to slice their way through the panic-stricken crowd.

"It is Filli!" gasped Barda. "They are afraid of Filli."

"Kill it!" howled the Ra-Kacharz. They were very close now.

Barda, Lief, and Jasmine looked around desperately. There was nowhere to run. A press of people struggled at every door, trying to get through.

"Run, Filli!" Jasmine cried in fear. "Run! Hide!"

She threw Filli to the floor and he darted away. The people screamed at the sight of him, stumbling back, falling and trampling one another in their terror. He scampered through the gap in the crowd and was gone.

But Lief, Barda, and Jasmine were trapped. And the Ra-Kacharz were upon them.

8 - The Trial

The great logs in the meeting hall fireplace had been lit, and the blaze threw a ghastly red light over the faces of the prisoners.

For hours they had stood there, while a useless search was made for Filli. The Ra-Kacharz guarded them grimly, their eyes growing darker and more stern as the minutes ticked by.

Exhausted and silent, Lief, Barda, and Jasmine awaited their fate. They had learned by now that it was useless to argue, rage, or plead. In bringing a furred animal into Noradz they had committed the most hideous of crimes.

Finally, Reece spoke.

"We can wait no longer. The trial must begin."

A gong sounded, and black-clad people began to file into the hall. They arranged themselves in rows, facing the prisoners. Lief saw that Tira, the serving girl he had saved from punishment, was in the first row, very near to him. He tried to meet her eyes, but she looked quickly at the ground.

Reece raised his voice so all could hear.

"Because of these unclean ones, evil is abroad in Noradz. They have broken our most sacred law. They claim it was done out of ignorance. I think they lie, and deserve death. Others of the Nine believe them, and think imprisonment should be their fate. Therefore, it will be left to the sacred Cup to decide."

Barda, Jasmine, and Lief stole glances at one another. What new madness was this?

Reece took from the shelf above the fireplace a shining silver goblet — once used for drinking wine, perhaps.

"The Cup reveals the truth," he droned. "Noradzeer."

"Noradzeer," murmured the watching people.

Next, Reece showed two small cards. Each card had one word printed upon it.

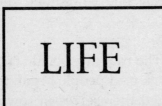 

He turned to the prisoners. "One among you will draw a card from the Cup," he said, his dark eyes gleaming. "Who will be that person?"

The companions hesitated. Then Lief stepped forward. "I will," he said reluctantly.

Reece nodded. "Face the front," he said briefly.

Lief did as he was told. Reece turned away from him, and from his fellow Ra-Kacharz. He put his gloved hand over the Cup.

Lief saw that Tira was watching Reece with close attention. Suddenly, her blue eyes widened with astonishment and horror. She glanced quickly at Lief, and her lips moved soundlessly.

Lief's face began to burn as he made out the mouthed words.

Both cards say "Death."

Tira must have seen Reece replace the "Life" card with a second "Death" card hidden in his sleeve or his glove. Reece was determined that the strangers would die.

The tall red figure turned back to him, the Cup held high. "Choose!" Reece sneered.

Lief did not know what to do. If he cried out that the Cup held only two "Death" cards, no one would believe him. Everyone would think that he was simply afraid to face the trial. No one would take his word, or Tira's, against the word of the First Ra-Kachar of Noradz. And Reece could easily change the cards around again if challenged.

Lief slipped his fingers under his shirt and gripped the topaz fixed to the Belt. It had helped him find answers before. Could it help him now? The fire roared behind him, lighting the tall figure in front of him with an eerie glow. The silver cup shone red like solid flame.

Flame. Fire . . .

His heart thudding, Lief stretched up his hand, dipped his fingers into the Cup, and chose a card. Then, like lightning, he whirled, seemed to stumble backwards, and dropped the card into the roaring flames. It flared for a moment, and was consumed.

"I beg pardon for my clumsiness," cried Lief, over the horrified gasps of the crowd. "But you can easily tell which card I drew. Simply look at the one remaining in the Cup."

Reece stood perfectly still, seething with baffled rage, as one of the other Ra-Kacharz took the Cup from his hand and plucked out the card that still lay within it. She held it up.

"The card that remains is 'Death,' " she droned. "The prisoner drew the 'Life' card. The Cup has spoken."

Lief felt Barda's hand grip his shoulder. Weak at the knees, he turned to face his friends. Their eyes were relieved, but full of questions. They suspected that he had burned the card on purpose, and wondered why.

"Take them to the dungeons," Reece thundered.

"There they will live out their lives, repenting of the evil they have done."

The eight other Ra-Kacharz surrounded Lief, Barda, and Jasmine and began marching them from the hall. The whispering crowd parted to let them through. Lief twisted his head, looking for Tira among the black-clad figures, but could not see her.

As they left the hall, they heard Reece's voice raised once more as he spoke to the people. "Continue the search for the creature who has befouled our city," he ordered. "It must be found and killed before night-fall."

Lief glanced at Jasmine. She did not open her lips, but her face was pale and set. He knew that she was thinking of Filli — hunted and afraid.

The Ra-Kacharz pushed their prisoners through a maze of brightly lit hallways and down some winding stone steps. The smell of soap hung everywhere, and the stones under their feet were scrubbed smooth.

At the bottom of the steps was a large space lined with metal doors, each with a narrow flap through which a tray of food could be passed. The leading Ra-Kachar threw one of the doors open, and her companions pulled Lief, Barda, and Jasmine to-wards it.

Jasmine took one look at the grim, windowless cell beyond the door and began to struggle wildly. Lief and Barda, too, fought grimly for their freedom. But it was no use. They had no weapons, no protection against the whips of the Ra-Kacharz, cracking around their faces, stinging their legs and arms. They were driven back into the cell. Then the door was slammed behind them and a heavy bolt was driven home.

They threw themselves at the door, beating on it with their fists. But the footsteps of the Ra-Kacharz were already fading into the distance.

Frantically, they searched the cell, looking for weaknesses. But the narrow wooden bunks fixed to one wall could not be moved. The empty water trough fixed to another wall was solid as rock.

"They will come back," Barda said grimly. "We were condemned to life, not death. They will have to give us food, and fill the water trough. They cannot leave us here to starve or die of thirst."

But miserable hours passed, and no one came.

✳

They had all drifted into an uneasy sleep when the scratching came at the door. Even when Lief woke, he thought he had dreamed the timid sound. But then it came again. He jumped from his bunk and ran to the door with Jasmine and Barda close behind him. The food flap had been pushed open. Through it, they could see the blue eyes of Tira.

"The First Ra-Kachar gave orders that he and he alone would bring you food and water," she whispered. "But — I feared that he may have . . . forgotten. Have you eaten? Has the water trough been filled?"

"No!" Lief whispered back. "And you know that he did not just forget, Tira. That is why you came. Reece intends us to die here."

"It cannot be!" Her voice was agonized. "The Cup gave you Life."

"Reece cares nothing for the Cup!" hissed Barda. "He cares only for his own will. Tira, unbolt the door! Let us out!"

"I cannot! I dare not! You brought evil to our halls, and it has still not been found. All except the night cooks are sleeping now. That is why I could slip away and not be missed. But the people are afraid, and many are crying out in their sleep. In the morning, the search will begin again." Through the narrow slit, the girl's eyes were dark with fear.

"Where we come from, animals like Filli are not evil," Lief said. "We meant no harm in bringing him here. He is Jasmine's friend. But if you do not let us out of this cell, we are doomed. Reece will see to it that we die of hunger and thirst and no one will ever know. No one but you."

There was no reply but a soft groan.

"Please help us!" begged Lief. "Tira, please!"

There was a moment's silence. Then the eyes disappeared and they heard the sliding of the bolt.

The door swung open and they crowded out of the cell. White-faced in the light of the torches, Tira gave them water and they drank thirstily. She said nothing as they thanked her, and when they bolted

61

the door behind them to disguise their escape, she shivered and covered her face with her hands. Plainly, she felt as though she was doing something very wrong.

But when they discovered their packs hidden in a crevice beside the stone steps, she gasped with surprise. "We were told that these had been put into your cell with you!" she said. "So that you would have bedding, and some comforts."

"Who told you that?" asked Barda grimly.

"The First Ra-Kachar," she whispered. "He said he had brought them to you himself."

"Well, he did not, as you can see," snapped Jasmine, pulling her bag onto her back.

They crept up the steps. The passage above was empty, but they could hear a few distant voices.

"We must escape the city," Barda whispered. "Which way should we go?"

"There is no way out." Tira shook her head hopelessly. "The gate in the hill is locked and barred. Those who work in the fields are taken out each morning and brought back at night. No one else may leave, on pain of death."

"There must be another way!" hissed Lief.

She hesitated, then shook her head. But Jasmine had seen the hesitation, and pounced.

"What did you think of, just then? Tell us what is in your mind!" she urged.

Tira licked her lips. "It is said . . . it is said that

the Hole leads, in the end, to the outside world. But — "

"What is the Hole?" demanded Barda. "Where is it?"

"It is near the kitchens," shuddered Tira. "It is where they throw the food that has not passed inspection. But it is — forbidden."

"Take us there!" hissed Jasmine fiercely. "Take us there now!"

9 - The Kitchens

They crept like thieves through the corridors, darting into side passages whenever they heard someone approaching. Finally they reached a small metal door.

"This leads to the walkways above the kitchens," Tira whispered. "The walkways are used by the Ra-Kacharz, to watch the work below, and by those whose task it is to wash the kitchen walls."

She opened the door a crack. From the space beyond poured the smell of cooking, and a muffled clattering.

"Be very silent," the girl breathed. "Tread softly. Then we will not be noticed. The night cooks work at speed. They have much to do before dawn."

She slipped through the door, and the companions followed her. The sight that met their eyes astonished them.

They were standing on a narrow metal walkway. Far below lay the great kitchens of Noradz, clattering with sound and blazing with light. The kitchens were huge — as big as a small village — and filled with working people dressed as Tira was, but all in gleaming white.

Some were peeling vegetables or preparing fruits. Others were mixing, baking, stirring pots that bubbled on the huge stoves. Thousands of cakes cooled on racks, waiting to be iced and decorated. Hundreds of pies and tarts were being lifted from the great ovens. At one side, a team was packing prepared foods into boxes and glass or stone jars.

"But — surely this does not go on every day and every night?" gasped Lief in amazement. "How much food can the people of Noradz eat?"

"Only a small amount of the food prepared is eaten," Tira whispered back. "Much of what is cooked does not pass the inspection and is wasted." She sighed. "The cooks are valued, trained from their youngest days, but I would not like to be one of them. It makes them sad to try so hard, and to fail so often."

They crept along the walkway, looking down, fascinated, at the activity below. They had been moving for about five minutes when Tira stopped and crouched.

"Ra-Kachaz!" she breathed.

Sure enough, two red-clad figures were striding into the kitchens.

"It is an inspection," whispered Tira.

The Ra-Kacharz moved quickly to a place where four cooks stood, their hands behind their backs. Hundreds of jars of sugared fruits, bright as jewels, were lined up on a counter, awaiting inspection.

The Ra-Kacharz paced along the line of jars, staring at them closely. When they had reached the end, they turned and paced back again. This time they pointed at certain jars, and these the cooks picked up and put on another bench.

When finally the inspection was finished, six jars of fruit had been separated from the rest.

"Those are the jars that will be blessed, and eaten by the people," said Tira. "The rest have been rejected." She gazed with sympathy at the cooks, who, shoulders sagging with disappointment, had begun packing the rejected jars into a huge metal bin.

Lief, Barda, and Jasmine stared, horrified. The fruit all looked delicious and wholesome to them. "This is wicked!" Lief muttered angrily, as the Ra-Kacharz turned and strode away to another part of the kitchens. "In Del, people are starving, scrabbling for scraps. And here, good food is wasted!"

Tira shook her head. "It is not good food," she insisted earnestly. "The Ra-Kacharz know when food is unclean. By their inspections the Ra-Kacharz protect the people from disease and illness. Noradzeer."

Lief would have liked to argue. Jasmine, too, was

red with anger. But Barda shook his head at them, warning them to be silent. Lief bit his lips. He knew that Barda was right. They needed Tira's help. There was no point in upsetting her. She was not to understand how things were in the rest of Deltora. She knew only her place, and the laws with which she had grown up.

In silence they moved on along the walkway and at last came to the end of the kitchens. Steep metal steps led down to the ground just in front of a door.

"The Hole is through that door," Tira said in a low voice. "But — "

She broke off and crouched once more, gesturing to her companions to do the same. The four cooks who had made the sugared fruits walked into view below, carrying the bin of rejected jars between them. The bin was now sealed tightly with a metal lid. They carried it through the door, and disappeared from sight.

"They are going to put the bin into the Hole," Tira whispered.

A few moments later the cooks came back and walked off to their part of the kitchens to begin the task of preparing food all over again. Tira, Lief, Barda, and Jasmine crept down the steps, passed shelves lined with pots and pans, and slipped through the door.

They found themselves in a small, bare room. To

their left was a red-painted door. Facing them, on the wall opposite the kitchens, a metal grille barred the round, dark entrance to the Hole.

"Where does the red door lead?" asked Barda.

"To the sleeping quarters of the Nine," Tira whispered. "They sleep in turns, it is said, coming through this door when inspections are due."

She glanced nervously over her shoulder. "Let us leave here, now. I brought you here because you demanded it. But at any moment we may be surprised."

The companions crept closer to the Hole and peered through the grille. Dimly they saw the beginning of a tunnel lined with stone that seemed to gleam red. The tunnel's roof and sides were rounded. It was very narrow, and sloped down into blackness. Deep within it, something growled, long and low.

"What is inside?" murmured Lief.

"We do not know," answered Tira. "Only the Ra-Kacharz can enter the Hole and survive."

"So they tell you!" said Lief scornfully.

But Tira shook her head. "In my life I have seen two people try to escape the city through the Hole," she said softly. "Both were brought out stiff and dead. Their eyes were open and staring. Their hands were torn and blistered. There was foam on their lips." She shuddered. "It is said that they died of terror."

The dull roar sounded again from the tunnel. They peered into its darkness, but could see nothing.

"Tira, do you know where our weapons are?"

asked Barda urgently. "The swords — and the daggers?"

Tira nodded warily. "They are waiting at the furnace," she whispered. "Tomorrow they will be melted down, to be made into new things for the kitchen."

"Get them for us!" Barda urged.

She shook her head. "I cannot!" she hissed desperately. "It is forbidden to touch them, and already I have committed terrible crimes for you."

"All we want is to leave here!" exclaimed Lief. "How can that hurt your people? And no one will ever know that it was you who helped us."

"Reece is the First of the Nine," murmured Tira. "His word is law."

"Reece does not deserve your loyalty," hissed Barda furiously. "You have seen for yourself that he lies and cheats, and makes a mockery of your laws! If anyone deserves to die, it is he!"

But in saying this, he had gone too far. Tira's cheeks flushed, her eyes widened, and she turned and ran back into the kitchen. The door swung closed behind her.

Barda sighed impatiently. "I frightened her," he muttered. "I should have guarded my tongue! What will we do now?"

"We will make the best of it." Determinedly, Lief lifted the grille from the tunnel entrance. "If the Ra-Kacharz can enter the Hole and live, so can we — with weapons or without."

He turned and beckoned to Jasmine. She backed away, shaking her head.

"I cannot go," she said loudly. "I thought Filli might be here, waiting for me. But he is not. He would not leave Noradz without me, and I will not leave without him."

Lief felt like shaking her. "Jasmine! There is no time to waste!" he urged. "Stop this foolishness!"

She turned her clear green gaze to him. "I am not asking you and Barda to remain," she said calmly. "You began this quest without me, and so you can continue." She looked away. "Perhaps — it may be better, in any case," she added.

"What do you mean?" Lief demanded. "Why would it be better?"

She shrugged. "We do not agree on — some things," she said. "I am not sure — "

But she never finished what she had to say, for at that moment the red door behind her burst open and Reece strode in, his black eyes glistening with triumphant fury. Before she could move he had grabbed her with one powerful arm and lifted her off her feet.

"So, girl!" he snarled in her ear. "My ears did not deceive me. By what witchcraft did you escape from your cell?"

Lief and Barda started towards him but he lashed out at them with his whip, holding them back.

"Spies!" he growled. "Now your wickedness is proved. Now you invade our kitchens — to guide your evil creature to them, no doubt. When the people hear this, they will be happy for you to die a thousand deaths."

Jasmine struggled, but his grip was like iron.

"You cannot escape, girl," he sneered. "Even now, others of the Nine are stirring beyond this door. Your friends will die before you. I trust you will enjoy hearing their screams."

He lashed at Lief and Barda with his whip, driving them back, slowly but surely, towards the Hole.

10 - The Hole

One thought burned in Lief's mind more strongly than all the rest. Some terrible danger really did lurk within the darkness of the Hole. Otherwise Reece would not be smiling so triumphantly as he drove his prisoners towards it.

Barda and Jasmine had plainly come to the same conclusion. Jasmine was shrieking, vainly tearing at the Ra-Kacharz' thick garments with her nails. Barda was struggling to hold his ground, his arms wrapped around his head to protect it.

The leather whip flicked viciously around Lief's ears. He staggered back, turning away, the stinging pain bringing tears to his eyes. Again the whip cracked, and now the warm blood was running down his neck and shoulders. The blackness of the Hole yawned just in front of him . . .

Then there was a dull, ringing thump. And suddenly there was no more cracking of the whip, no more stinging pain.

Lief spun around.

Tira was standing over Reece's crumpled body. The kitchen door gaped wide behind her. Her eyes were glazed with fear. In her left hand she clutched the companions' weapons. In her right was the frying pan she had snatched from the kitchen shelf and used to hit Reece over the head.

With a gasp of horror at what she had done, she threw the pan violently away from her. It struck the stones with a ringing crash.

Lief, Barda, and Jasmine raced to the girl's side and took their weapons from her. She seemed paralyzed with shock. She had sprung to their defense without thinking, but plainly in attacking a Ra-Kachar she had committed a terrible crime.

"Barda!" hissed Jasmine urgently. She pointed. The handle of the red door was turning.

Barda flung himself against the door and leaned against it with all his strength. Jasmine added her weight to his. An angry thumping began and the door shuddered.

"Run, Tira!" hissed Lief. "Go! Forget this ever happened."

She stared at him, wild-eyed. He hurried her towards the kitchen door, pushed her through, and shot the bolt behind her. Now the Ra-Kacharz trying to beat their way through the red door would have no help from the people in the kitchen, and, with luck, Tira would be able to reach the stairs and climb to the walkway unseen.

He spun around again just in time to see Barda and Jasmine knocked sprawling and the red door flying open. He sprang to his friends' aid, and, at the same moment, three Ra-Kacharz charged through the opening. Though they had been roused from sleep, they were fully dressed in their red suits, gloves, and boots, and their heads and faces were covered.

Their eyes were already burning with rage as they burst into the little room. But when they saw their leader lying on the floor, and the three prisoners standing over him, they roared and lunged forward, cracking their whips without mercy.

Barda, Lief, and Jasmine were driven back, their blades slashing uselessly at the empty air. Lief cried out in frustration as a whip curled around his sword and tore it out of his hand.

Now he was helpless. In moments he heard with horror the sound of Barda's sword, too, clattering to the ground. Now Jasmine's two daggers were their only defense. But the Ra-Kacharz were pushing forward, driving them into a corner, the lashing whips whirling together in the air like a terrible, cutting machine.

"Stop!" cried Jasmine piercingly. "We mean you no harm! We want only to leave this place!"

Her voice echoed against the stone walls, soaring above the cracking of the whips. The Ra-Kacharz did not falter. They made no sign that they had even heard.

But someone had heard. Through the red door hurtled a scrap of grey fur, chattering and squeaking with joy.

"Filli!" exclaimed Jasmine.

The Ra-Kacharz shouted in horror and disgust, lurching out of the way as the little animal scuttled between them, leaping for Jasmine's shoulder.

It was just a moment's distraction, but it was all that Barda needed. With a roar he hurled himself at the two nearest red-clad figures, throwing them against the wall with all his strength. Their heads hit the stones and they slumped together to the ground.

Lief twisted and kicked at the third Ra-Kachar, feeling his foot connect with the leg just above the boot. The man howled and stumbled. Lief snatched up the frying pan and felled him with a single blow.

Panting above the bodies of their fallen enemies, the friends glanced over to where Jasmine stood, crooning to Filli.

"Filli saved us," Jasmine said happily. "How brave he is! He was lost, but he heard my voice and came running to me. Poor Filli. He has been so afraid, and in such danger!"

"*He* has been afraid and in danger!" exploded Barda. "And what of us?"

But Jasmine simply shrugged and went back to stroking Filli's fur.

"What are we to do now?" muttered Lief. "There are four Ra-Kacharz here, counting Reece. And we know that there are two in the kitchens. But three of the Nine are still missing. Where are they? Where should we go for safety?"

"We must take our chances with the tunnel," said Barda grimly, looking around for his sword. "There is no other way out for us."

Lief glanced at the Hole. "Reece thought that whatever is in there would kill us," he said.

"If the Ra-Kacharz can survive it, so can we," snapped Barda. "They are strong, and good fighters, but they do not have magic powers."

"We should put on their garments," said Jasmine from her place by the wall. "Surely it is not by chance that they dress differently from the others in this place, and it is only they who can use the Hole. Perhaps the creature that dwells in the darkness is trained to attack all colors but red."

Barda nodded slowly. "It could be. In any case, to wear the Ra-Kacharz garments is a good idea," he said. "Our own clothes mark us as strangers. We could never bluff our way out of the city through the front entrance. But perhaps the back way . . ."

They wasted no more time, but began to strip the three Ra-Kacharz they had just defeated. Jasmine was quick and deft at the work. Lief could not help remembering, with a chill, how many times she had stripped the bodies of Grey Guards in the Forests of

Silence. She had done it to obtain clothes and other things she needed, and she had done it efficiently and without a moment's pity, as she was doing now.

They dressed quickly, pulling the red garments over their own clothes, the boots over their own shoes. The Ra-Kacharz lay still. Tight white underclothes covered them from wrist to ankle. Their heads, like those of the other people in the city, were shaved bald.

"They do not look so dangerous now," said Jasmine grimly, winding red cloth around her head and making sure that Filli was buttoned securely under the collar of her clothes.

Despite his haste and worry, Lief had to smile as he glanced at her. She looked very strange. The Ra-Kacharz garments were too big for him and even for Barda, but on Jasmine they hung in vast, baggy folds. The gloves were not a problem, for they were made of a clinging material that fitted all sizes. But he doubted that she would be able to walk in the huge red boots.

Jasmine had thought of that. Carrying the boots in her hand, she ran over to where Reece lay. She pulled off his gloves, crumpled them, and stuffed them into the toe of one boot. Then she unwound the cloth that bound his head and face and used it in the second boot.

Reece mumbled, his shaven head rolling on the hard floor.

"He is waking," Jasmine said, pulling on the

boots. She drew the dagger from her belt.

"Do not kill him!" exclaimed Lief in panic.

Jasmine glanced at him in surprise. "Why not?" she demanded. "He would kill me, if our places were reversed. And when he was attacking you, you would have killed him, if you could."

Lief could not explain. He knew she would never agree that to kill in the heat of the moment, in defense of your life, was very different from killing a man, even an enemy, in cold blood.

But Barda had suddenly exclaimed, striding to Jasmine's side. He crouched beside Reece's body. "Look at this!" he muttered, pushing the man's head to one side.

Lief knelt beside him. On the side of Reece's neck was the ugly scar of an old burn. The scar was in a shape he knew only too well.

"He has been branded," he hissed, looking at the dull red mark with horror. "Branded with the mark of the Shadow Lord. Yet he lives here, free and powerful. What does this mean?"

"It means that things in Noradz are not what they seem," said Barda grimly. Quickly he moved to the bodies of the other Ra-Kacharz. The Shadow Lord's brand was on every one.

They looked up sharply as the handle of the door that led into the kitchen shook and rattled. There was a loud knock. Someone was trying to get in.

"Another inspection must have been completed," muttered Jasmine. "The cooks have a bin of food to throw away."

Finding that their way was barred, the people behind the door began shouting and thumping with their fists. Reece mumbled and groaned. His eyelids fluttered. He was about to wake.

Barda sprang to his feet. "We will take him with us. We will force him to tell us how to save ourselves from whatever is inside the passage. And, in any case, a hostage will be useful."

Hastily they pulled their packs onto their backs and dragged Reece to the Hole entrance. They pushed him into the darkness. Then, one by one, they crawled after him. There was no time, now, to think of what might await them below.

11 - The Price of Freedom

Lief slithered cautiously down the slope, holding Reece's ankles with one gloved hand, and with the other catching at the sides and roof of the passage to stop himself from moving too quickly. It was not easy, for the rock was covered with a thin layer of fungus that slipped and smeared under his fingers. Gradually the passage narrowed until it was just wide enough for one of the big bins to move through without sticking.

Lief's pack kept catching on the roof. With a shout of warning to Barda, who was behind him, he wriggled till the straps slipped from his shoulders, and let himself slide away from underneath the bag. He knew that it would keep moving after him. The slope had become steeper, and it was all he could do to stop himself from slipping down out of control.

Other things had changed, too. The growling was louder, a ceaseless rumbling that seemed to fill Lief's ears and his mind. It was harder to hold Reece, who was still not quite awake, but was starting to move his legs, to catch at the walls with his hands, and to raise his head so that now and then it grazed the roof of the tunnel.

And there was light below — a faint glow, too yellow to be moonlight. It quickly grew brighter and Lief realized that he was reaching the bottom of the slope, that the passage was about to level out.

"Be ready!" he shouted to Barda and Jasmine. And almost at the same moment, without warning, Reece's body began to writhe and twist. He shrieked and kicked. His ankles slipped from Lief's grasp and he slid away, downward towards the light. Gasping with shock, Lief saw his jerking body reach the bottom of the slope.

But it did not stop. Somehow, it kept moving.

Thinking of nothing but keeping his enemy in sight, Lief let go of the walls and let himself slide down the last part of the slope. In moments he had reached level ground.

Ahead of him the passage broadened. Light glowed softly from the roof. The rumbling sound was all about him. The ground beneath him was no longer the smooth, hard rock of the tunnel, but something softer, lumpier — something that trembled slightly under his hands . . . and that moved! Like Reece, he was being carried on — and the ground itself was carrying him!

The red-clad figure was crawling a little further ahead. Lief picked himself up and ran towards it, covering the distance in seconds. He jumped for the writhing man, wrestling with him, trying to hold him still.

Their rolling, struggling bodies hit the wall at the side of the passage. Lief felt rough earth beneath him. Rough earth that did not rumble or move. Reece arched his back, cried out, and lay still.

Then Lief realized two things. The center of the passage was a moving path, driven by some unseen machinery. And Reece was dead. Horribly dead. Lief gazed down at the terrible face, and shuddered, remembering Tira's description of others who had tried to escape through the Hole.

He heard a shout and saw Barda and Jasmine running towards him down the pathway, looming out of the darkness with amazing speed.

"Jump off to the side!" Lief called. "The moving strip is only in the center!"

They did as he told them, stumbling as their feet hit solid ground. When they reached his side, and saw Reece's body, they gasped in horror.

"What — what has happened to him?" muttered Barda, shuddering.

The palms of the man's hands, and the top of his

shaved skull, were smeared with red fungus, and hideously blistered. Foam flecked his lips. His face was blue, twisted into a grimace of agony.

"Poison!" breathed Jasmine. She looked feverishly around her. "In the Forests of Silence there is a spider whose bite can — "

"There are no spiders here," Lief broke in, his stomach churning. His finger shook slightly as he pointed to the dead man's head and hands. "The fungus in the passage — I think — I think one touch on bare skin is deadly. We dragged Reece to his death. He woke, and saw where he was. But already it was too late."

Sickened, they looked down at the crumpled body. "I did not know," Jasmine said, defiantly, at last. "I did not know that to take his gloves and the wrapping from his head would kill him!"

"Of course you did not," said Barda quietly. "How could you? Only the Ra-Kacharz know that it is their gloves and head-coverings that allow them to enter the Hole and live." He grimaced. "Our clothes are smeared all over with the fungus. How will we be able to take them off in safety?"

Lief had been thinking about that.

"I think that the poison is only deadly when it is fresh," he muttered, looking down at his own gloved hands. "I do not see how, otherwise, the Ra-Kacharz could go among their people without harming them."

Barda shrugged. "I pray that you are right."

There was a soft sound behind them. They spun around and saw the gleaming shape of one of the silver drums sliding down the Hole and coming to rest on the moving pathway. It settled gently and began to come towards them.

"I closed the grille after us, hoping that the cooks would not realize that we had escaped into the Hole," said Jasmine. "It seems they have not."

"Not yet," said Barda grimly. "But once the Ra-Kacharz' sleeping quarters have been searched, they will know there was nowhere else for us to go. We must find the way out quickly. If we follow this tunnel, I believe we will find ourselves on the other side of the hill."

Leaving Reece's body where it lay, they jumped back onto the moving pathway and began running along it, soon leaving the silver drum far behind them.

They had not been travelling for long when they saw a gleam ahead of them, felt fresh air on their faces, and heard the sound of clangs and voices. They jumped from the moving pathway again and began creeping along beside it, flattening themselves against the tunnel wall.

It grew lighter. The voices grew louder. There were strange, snuffling sounds, too — sounds that seemed familiar to Lief, though he could not place them. And then, all at once, he saw a gateway ahead. The moving pathway stopped just in front of it, and a small cluster of the silver bins stood in the opening like guards. Beyond them Lief could see the shapes of trees, and grey sky. A night bird called. It was nearly dawn.

As he watched, three tall figures strode into view. Each lifted one of the bins, and carried it out of sight.

"They were Ra-Kacharz!" hissed Jasmine. "Did you see?"

Lief nodded in puzzlement. So the three missing Ra-Kacharz were here. What were they doing with the waste food? And what was that snuffling sound? He had definitely heard it before. But where?

The three companions crept forward, keeping low and close to the wall, craning their necks to see through the gateway. But when at last the scene outside lay before their eyes, they stopped dead, gaping with astonishment.

The Ra-Kacharz were lifting the bins onto a cart, carefully packing straw between them so they would not rattle together. Two other carts stood waiting, already fully loaded. And snuffling happily between the shafts of each cart was — a muddlet!

"They are taking the bins away! And they are using our muddlets to do it!" Lief whispered.

Jasmine shook her head. "I do not think they are our beasts," she breathed. "They look very like them, but their color patches are in different places." She

peered around the corner of the gateway and stiffened. "There is a whole field of muddlets just over
there," she hissed. "There must be twenty of them!"

Barda shook his head. "Our beasts are probably
among them," he said grimly. "But they can stay
there. I would not ride a muddlet again if my life de-
pended upon it."

"Well, our lives *do* depend on our getting away
from here as fast as we can," muttered Jasmine. "What
do you think we should do?"

Barda and Lief exchanged glances. The same
thought was in both their minds.

"The straw between the bins is deep," said Lief.
"We could hide in it well enough, I think."

Barda nodded. "So, history will repeat itself,
Lief." He grinned. "We will escape from here in the
same way your father escaped from the palace in Del
as a boy. In a rubbish cart!"

"But what of Kree?" Jasmine whispered. "How
will he know where I am?"

As if in answer to her question, there was a
screech from one of the trees. Jasmine's face bright-
ened.

"He is here!" she hissed.

At that moment the Ra-Kacharz came back to
carry away more bins and the companions moved out
of sight. But as soon as the red-clad figures had staggered away with their huge burdens, three shadows
darted from the shelter of the gateway and climbed

into one of the loaded carts. One of them signalled at the trees as she burrowed under the straw between the bins, and a bird cried out in answer.

The friends lay cramped, still, and hidden while the Ra-Kacharz finished their work.

"Was that the last?" they heard a familiar voice ask. It was the woman who had spoken for them at the trial.

"It seems so," said another voice. "I had thought there would be more. There must be a problem in the kitchens. But we can wait no longer, or we will be late."

Late? Lief thought, suddenly alert. Late for what?

There was a creaking sound as the Ra-Kacharz climbed into the carts. Then three voices cried, "Brix!" and with a jolt the carts started to move.

Lying under the straw, the three companions could see nothing but patches of grey sky, and, now and then, the shape of Kree flying high above them. If the Ra-Kacharz thought it strange that a raven should be flying before dawn, they said nothing. Perhaps, Lief thought, they did not even notice Kree, so intent were they on urging the muddlets to greater speed.

Lief, Barda, and Jasmine had planned to jump from the cart when they were a safe distance from the city. But they had not counted upon their cart being in the middle of the three. And they had not counted upon the speed of the muddlets.

The carts jolted and bounced upon the rough roads, and the countryside flew by. Even dragging heavy loads, the beasts galloped amazingly fast. It was plain that any attempt to jump would lead to injury and capture.

"We will have to wait until the carts stop," whispered Jasmine. "Surely they cannot be going far."

But the minutes stretched into hours, and dawn had broken, before finally the carts slowed and jolted to a halt. And when, sleepy and confused, Lief peered cautiously through the straw to see where they were, his stomach seemed to turn over.

They were back at Tom's shop. And marching towards them was a troop of Grey Guards.

12 – A Matter of Business

The carts creaked as the drivers climbed from their seats and jumped to the ground. "You are late!" growled the leader of the Grey Guards.

"It could not be helped," said one of the Ra-Kacharz calmly. Lief heard a jingling sound, and guessed that the muddlets were being freed from their harness.

There was the sound of hooves, as though horses were being led towards the carts. The grey horses from the field behind the shop, Lief thought.

"Good morrow, my lords and my lady Ra-Kacharz!" shouted Tom's voice. "A fine day!"

"A fine day to be late!" the Guard grumbled.

"Leave this to me, my friend," said Tom heartily. "I will see to the changing of the beasts. Go and finish your ale. It is a long, dry way back to Del."

Lief's heart lurched. He heard Barda and Jasmine draw quick, horrified breaths.

The food was not to be dumped. The carts were going on to Del!

Lief lay motionless, his mind whirling. He hardly heard the sounds of the Guards' feet marching back to the shop. Suddenly, everything had fallen into place. For centuries carts had trundled up the hill to the palace in Del, loaded with luxurious foods. However scarce food was in the city, the favored people of the palace never went hungry.

No one had ever known where the food came from. But now Lief did.

The food came from Noradz. The people of Noradz labored to grow and gather food in their fertile fields. The cooks of Noradz worked night and day to produce delicious dishes. But only a little of what they made was enjoyed by their people. The rest was taken all the way to the palace in Del. Once it had kept the kings and queens of Deltora in ignorance of their people's misery. Now it fed the servants of the Shadow Lord.

The Ra-Kacharz were traitors to their people. Tom, who had pretended to be against the Shadow Lord, was in fact a friend to the Grey Guards.

A hot wave of anger flooded Lief. But Barda had his mind on more pressing matters.

"We must get out of this cart!" he hissed. "Now, while the Guards are gone. Lief, can you see — ?"

"I can see nothing!" Lief whispered back.

Harness jingled. Kree screeched from somewhere nearby.

"It is strange. That black bird has followed us all the way from Noradz," said a Ra-Kachar's voice.

"Indeed," said Tom thoughtfully.

Lief, Barda, and Jasmine stiffened under their covering of straw. Tom had seen Kree before. Would he guess . . . ?

Tom cleared his throat. "By the by, I must give you bad news. You will have to return to Noradz on foot. The fresh beasts kept here for your journey home have been stolen — by some crafty travellers."

"We know it!" said one of the Ra-Kacharz angrily. "You should have taken more care. We found the beasts trying to get back into their field behind the hill late yesterday. They had bolted for home, and thrown the strangers from their backs outside our front gate."

"The strangers brought evil to our halls," another Ra-Kachar droned. "They escaped death by a breath, and even now lie in our dungeons."

"Indeed," said Tom again, very softly. Then his voice became more cheerful. "There! These poor, tired muddlets are free from their bonds. If you will take them to the field, I will finish harnessing the horses. Then, perhaps, you will share a mug of ale with me before you begin your march."

The Ra-Kacharz agreed, and soon Lief, Barda,

and Jasmine heard the sound of the muddlets being led away.

Moments later, Tom spoke again. It seemed he was talking to the horses. "Should anyone wish to leave a cart unobserved, and run to the trees at the side of the shop, this would be the time to do it. Poor Tom is alone here, now."

The message was clear. Clumsily, the three companions wriggled out of the straw and ran, feeling stiff and bruised, to the shelter of the trees. Tom did not look up. He just went on harnessing the horses, whistling softly to himself.

Lief, Barda, and Jasmine lay watching as the shopkeeper walked casually to the back of the cart where they had been hiding and picked up the straw that had fallen to the ground. He pushed it back into place, then strolled towards the trees, his hands in his pockets. He bent down and began pulling grass, as though he was gathering it for the horses.

"You sold us muddlets that did not belong to you!" Barda hissed at him furiously.

"Ah well," murmured Tom, without looking up. "Poor Tom finds it hard to resist gold. He admits it. But what happened was your fault, not mine, my friend. If you had taken the left-hand path, as I advised, the beasts would never have caught the scent of home and bolted. You have only yourselves to blame for your present trouble."

"Perhaps we do," said Lief bitterly. "But at least our only crime is foolishness. You, however, are a liar. You pretend to be on the side of those who would resist the Shadow Lord, and all the time you help to feed his servants. You deal with Grey Guards as friends."

Tom straightened, a clump of sweet grass in his hand, and turned to look at the sign that rose so proudly upon his roof.

"Have you not noticed, my friend?" he said. "Tom's name looks the same, whichever side you are on. It is the same whether you approach from the west or the east. It is the same whether you are inside his shop, or outside it, whether you see it in a mirror, or with your own eyes. And Tom himself is like his name. It is a matter of business."

"Business?" spat Lief.

"Certainly. I am the same Tom to all. I do not take sides. I do not interest myself in things that are not my affair. This is wise, in these hard times. And there is far more money in it."

He smiled, the edges of his wide mouth curving up, creasing his thin face. "Now, I suggest you make haste to leave this place. I will keep my good friends the Ra-Kacharz here for as long as I can, to give you a good start. Take off those glaring red garments first, but do not leave them here, I beg you. I want no trouble."

He turned away and began strolling back towards the carts.

"You are a deceiver!" Lief hissed after him.

Tom paused. "Perhaps," he drawled, without looking back. "But I am a live, rich one. And because of me, you live to fight another day."

He walked on, holding out the grass and clicking his tongue to the horses.

The three friends began pulling off the red garments and boots, and stuffing them into their packs. Lief was simmering with rage. Jasmine glanced at him curiously.

"Tom helped us," she pointed out. "Why should you ask any more of him? Many creatures believe in nothing but themselves. He is one of those."

"Tom is not a creature, but a man," Lief snapped. "He should know what is right!"

"Are you so sure *you* know?" Jasmine answered sharply.

Lief stared at her. "What do you mean by that?" he demanded.

"Do not argue," said Barda wearily. "Save your strength for walking. It is a long way to Broad River." He fastened his pack, slung it over his shoulder, and tramped off through the trees.

"We must go back to Noradz first," said Lief, hurrying after him. "We must tell the people that they are being lied to!"

"Indeed?" said Barda wearily. "And if we survived long enough to tell them, which we probably would not, and if they believed us, which I do not think they would, and if by some miracle they broke the pattern of centuries, rebelled against the Ra-Kacharz, and refused to send their food away any longer . . . what do you think would happen?"

"The Shadow Lord's food supply would dry up," said Lief promptly.

"Yes. And then the Shadow Lord would bring down his wrath on Noradz, make the people do his will by force instead of by trickery, and begin scouring the country for us," said Barda bluntly. "Nothing would be gained, and much would be lost. It would be a disaster."

He lengthened his stride, and moved ahead.

Lief and Jasmine went after him, but they did not speak for a long time after that. Lief was too angry, and Jasmine's mind was busy with thoughts she did not wish to share.

13 - Broad River and Beyond

Four days of hard marching followed — four long days in which Lief, Barda, and Jasmine spoke little and then only of moving on and keeping out of sight of any possible enemy. But when, at last, in the afternoon of the fourth day, they stood on the banks of Broad River, they realized that they should have planned their next step more carefully.

The river was deep, and its name described it well. It was so wide that they could only faintly see the land on the other side. The great sheet of water stretched in front of them like a sea. There was no way across.

Bleached white, and hard as stone, the ancient remains of wooden rafts lay half-buried in the sand. Perhaps, long ago, people had crossed the river here, and abandoned the rafts where they came to rest. But there were no trees on this side to provide wood for rafts — only banks of reeds.

Jasmine's eyes narrowed as she peered across the dull sheen of the water. "The land on the other side is very flat," she said slowly. "It is a plain. And I see a dark shape rising from it. If that is the City of the Rats, it is straight ahead of us. All we have to do is — "

"Cross the river," said Lief heavily. He threw himself down on the fine, white sand and began rummaging in his pack, looking for something to eat.

He pulled out the collection of things they had bought from Tom and tipped them onto the ground in a small heap. He had almost forgotten about them, and now he stared at them with distaste.

They had seemed so exciting in the shop. Now they looked like rubbishy novelties. The beads that made fire. The "No Bakes" bread. The powder labelled "Pure and Clear." The little pipe that was supposed to blow bubbles of light. And a small, flat tin box with a faded label . . .

Of course. Tom's free gift. Something completely useless, no doubt, that he could not dispose of any other way. Lief sneered to himself as he turned the tin over.

"It is too far for us to swim. We will have to follow the river until we find a village where there are boats," Barda was saying. "It is a pity to have to go out of our way, but we have no choice."

"Perhaps we do," Lief said slowly.

Jasmine and Barda looked at him in surprise. He held up the box and read aloud the words on the back.

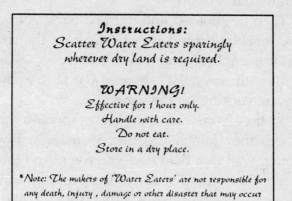

Instructions:
Scatter Water Eaters sparingly
wherever dry land is required.

WARNING!
Effective for 1 hour only.
Handle with care.
Do not eat.
Store in a dry place.

*Note: The makers of 'Water Eaters' are not responsible for
any death, injury, damage or other disaster that may occur
before, during or after the use of this product.

"Are you saying that whatever is in this little tin box can dry up a river?" jeered Jasmine.

Lief shrugged. "I am saying nothing. I am simply reading the instructions."

"There are more warnings than instructions," said Barda. "But we shall see."

They walked together to the river's edge and

Lief pried the lid off the tin box. Inside were some tiny crystals, each not much larger than a grain of sand. Feeling rather foolish, he pinched out a few of the crystals and tossed them into the water. They sank immediately without changing appearance in any way.

And nothing else happened.

Lief waited for a moment, then, fighting his disappointment, he tried to grin. "I should have known better," he shrugged. "As if that Tom would give away anything that actually — "

Then he shouted and jumped back. A huge, colorless, wobbling lump was rising from the river. Beside it was another — and another!

"It is the crystals!" shouted Barda in excitement. "They are sucking up the water!"

So they were. As they grew, spreading as Lief watched, they joined together to make a towering, wobbling wall that held back the river. And the water between them simply dried up, leaving a narrow, winding path of puddled, sandy mud.

Kree squawked in amazement as Jasmine, Lief, and Barda stepped carefully onto the riverbed, squeezing between the jellied lumps and walking on until they came to the end of the dry patch. Then Lief threw another pinch of crystals into the water ahead, and, after a moment, more lumps broke the surface of the river and another path began to clear for them.

✳

The crossing of Broad River was a strange, frightening journey. In all their minds was the thought of what would happen if the trembling walls that held back the river should fail. The great press of water would close over them. There would be no escape.

The swollen Water Eaters blocked their view as they crept along, twisting and turning, their feet sinking into the soft mud. Lief was just beginning to worry that the crystals in the tin box would run out before they reached the shore, when suddenly the shore was before him, and he was clambering up onto a harsh, dry plain.

He stood with Barda and Jasmine, staring.

The plain lay in the bend of the river. It was encircled by water on three sides, and should have been lush and fertile. But not a blade of grass softened its hard, baked clay. As far as the eye could see there was no sign of any living, growing thing.

In the center was a city whose towers shone dark red in the last rays of the setting sun. Though it was so far away, a feeling of evil and menace seemed to stream from it like vapor.

They left the river and began to move over the bare plain. The sky arched over them, red and lowering. From above, thought Lief suddenly, we must look like ants — three tiny, crawling ants. One blow would kill us all. Never had he felt so exposed to danger.

Kree felt it, too. He sat motionless on Jasmine's

shoulder. Filli was huddled inside her jacket, only his small nose visible. But even their company could not help Jasmine. Her feet dragged. She began to walk more and more slowly, and at last, as the sun began to sink below the horizon, she shuddered and stopped.

"I am sorry," she muttered. "The barrenness of this place is death to me. I cannot bear it."

Her face was white and set. Her hands were shaking. Lief and Barda glanced at each other.

"Only now I was thinking that we should soon stop for the night," said Barda, though Lief doubted this was true. "We must rest, and eat. And I do not think the city is a place to enter in darkness."

They sat down together and began unpacking their food, but there were no sticks to make a fire.

"Now is a good time to try Tom's fire-making beads," said Lief, following Barda's lead and trying to be cheerful. In the failing light, he read the instructions on the jar. Then he put one of the beads on the ground and hit it sharply with their digging tool. Immediately, it burst into flames. Lief added another bead and it, too, flared up. Soon there was a merry blaze that apparently needed no other fuel. He pushed the jar into his pocket, well-satisfied.

"Instant comfort. Amazing!" said Barda heartily. "A villain Tom may be, but at least the things he sells are worth their price."

It was still early, but Barda and Lief spread their

supplies around them and made much of deciding what they would eat. They added water to one of the flat white rounds of No Bakes and watched it swell quickly into a loaf of bread. They cut the bread into slices and toasted it, eating it with some of the dried berries, nuts, and honey they had carried from Raladin.

"A feast," said Barda contentedly, and Lief was relieved to see that Jasmine's tense face was beginning to relax. As they had hoped, the warmth, light, and food were giving her comfort.

He gazed over her shoulder at the distant city. The red light was fading from its towers now. Hulked on the plain, it stood silent, grim, deserted. . . .

Lief blinked. The last rays of the sun were playing tricks with his eyes. For a moment it had seemed as though the earth around the city were moving like water.

He looked again, and frowned in puzzlement. The plain *was* moving. Yet there was no grass to bend in the wind. No leaves to blow across the clay. What . . . ?

Then, suddenly, he saw. "Barda!" he said huskily.

He saw Barda look up, surprised by the fear in his voice. He tried to speak, but his breath caught in his throat. Waves of horror flooded through him as he stared wildly at the moving plain.

"What is it?" asked Jasmine, turning to look.

And then she and Barda were crying out together, leaping to their feet.

Spilling from the city, covering the ground, surging towards them like a long, low wave, was a scurrying, seething mass of rats.

14 - Night of the Rats

Rats in the thousands — in the tens of thousands! Suddenly Lief understood why the earth of the plain was bare. The rats had eaten every living thing.

They were creatures of the shadows. They had remained hidden in the ruined city while the sun glared down on the plain. But now they were coming, racing towards the scent of food in a frenzy of hunger.

"The river!" shouted Barda.

They ran for their lives. Lief glanced over his shoulder once only, and the sight he saw was enough to make him run even faster, gasping with fear.

The first rats had reached their campfire. They were huge. They were surging over the food and other belongings left scattered upon the ground, gobbling and tearing with needle-sharp teeth. But their fellows were close behind, leaping on top of them, smothering them, fighting one another for the spoils, tipping into the fire in the haste, squealing and shrieking.

And in the thousands more were scrambling over them, or wheeling around the struggling pile and scuttling on, sharp noses sniffing, black eyes gleaming. They could smell Lief, Barda, and Jasmine ahead — smell their warmth and their life and their fear.

Lief ran, the breath aching in his chest, his eyes fixed on the river. The water gleamed in the last rays of the sun. Nearer . . . nearer . . .

Jasmine was beside him, Barda close behind. Lief plunged into the cold water, gasping, and waded out as far as he dared. He turned to face the land, his cloak swirling around him.

The squealing, dark grey tide that was the rats reached the riverbank. Then it seemed to curl and break like a wave, and surged out into the water.

"They are swimming for us!" Barda shouted, struggling to draw his sword and pull it to the surface. "By the heavens, will nothing stop them?"

Already, Jasmine was slashing with her dagger, shouting fiercely, and dead rats in their dozens were being swept away by the tide. Beside her, Lief and Barda swept their blades across the water, back and forth, gasping with the effort of the task.

The water around them swirled with blood and foam. And still the rats came, clambering with bared teeth over their own sinking dead.

How long will our strength last? thought Lief. How long will it be before they overwhelm us?

His mind raced as he fought, his hands numb on the hilt of his sword. They would be safe on the other side of the river. The water was too wide for the rats to swim. But it was too wide for him, Jasmine, and Barda also. They would never survive if they cast themselves adrift in this cold, deep water.

And the long night was ahead. Until the sun rose again, bringing light to the plain, the rats would attack. Thousands would die, but thousands would take their places. Gradually Lief, Barda, and Jasmine would weaken. And then at last the rats would swarm over them, biting and clawing, till they sank beneath the water and drowned together.

The sun had set, and the plain had darkened. Lief could no longer see the city. All he could see was the campfire, flickering like a beacon.

It was then that he remembered that he had put the jar of fire beads in his pocket.

He took his left hand from his sword, plunged it under the water, and dug deep into his jacket. His fingers closed around the jar and he pulled it up to the surface. Water dripped from it, but the beads still rattled inside.

Shouting to Barda and Jasmine to cover him, he waded forward, unscrewing the jar's tight cap. He dug out a handful of beads with his stiff fingers and threw them at the rats on the bank with all his strength.

There was a huge burst of flame as the beads struck. The light was blinding. Hundreds of rats fell dead, killed by the sudden heat. The horde behind them shrieked, and scattered from the burning bodies. The creatures already in the water scrambled and writhed in terror, leaping towards Lief, Barda, and Jasmine, their long tails switching and coiling. Barda and Jasmine slashed at them, defending Lief and themselves, as Lief threw another handful of beads, and another, moving slowly downstream to lengthen the wall of flame.

And soon a long sheet of fire burned on the river's edge. Behind it the plain seethed. But where Lief, Barda, and Jasmine stood, panting and shuddering with relief, there was only rippling water, alive with red, leaping light. Dead rats were swept away by the tide, but no more took their places.

In a few moments there were splashes up and downstream as the rats began plunging into the river above and below the line of flame. But the distance was too great for them to swim in safety. The swift-running current pulled most of them under before they could reach their prey, and those that remained alive were easily beaten off.

So the three companions stood together, waist-deep in water, trembling with weariness but safe behind their fiery barricade, as the long, cold hours passed.

✳

Dawn broke at last. Dull red tinged the sky. Beyond the line of fire a murmuring, scuffling sound arose, like a forest of leaves rustling. Then it was gone, and a great stillness fell over the plain.

Lief, Barda, and Jasmine waded to the shore. Water streamed from their clothes and hair, hissing as it fell onto the flames of their barricade. They stepped over the flickering embers.

The rats had gone. Between the river and the smoking remains of the campfire there was nothing but a tangled litter of small bones.

"They have eaten their own dead," muttered Barda, looking sick.

"Of course," said Jasmine matter-of-factly.

Shivering with cold, feeling as though his legs were weighed down with stones, Lief began trudging towards the place where they had eaten their food many hours ago. Jasmine and Barda followed him, quiet and watchful. Kree flew overhead, the sound of his beating wings loud in the silent air.

Little remained around the ashes of the fire except for three patches of brilliant red.

Lief laughed shortly. "They have left the Ra-Kachar garments and boots," he said. "They did not like them, it seems. Why would that be?"

"Perhaps the garments still bear the scent of the fungus from the Hole," Jasmine suggested. "We can smell nothing — but we do not have the senses of a rat."

They looked around at the wreckage. Buckles from the packs, the caps of the water bags, the pipe that blew bubbles of light, a button or two, a few coins, and the flat tin box containing the last of the Water Eaters lay strewn on the hard clay among the bones and cinders. Except for the clothes from Noradz, nothing else had survived the rats' hunger. Not a crumb of food, a shred of blanket, or a thread of rope.

"At least we have our lives," said Barda, shivering in the light dawn breeze. "And we have dry garments to put on. They may not be the garments we would like, but who is to see us here?"

Wearily they stripped off their wet clothes and pulled on the red suits and boots of the Ra-Kacharz. Then, warm and dry at last, they sat down to talk.

"The jar of fire beads is almost empty. We will not survive another night on this plain," said Barda heavily. "We must enter the city now, if we are to enter it at all. These strange garments will give us some protection, since the rats do not like them. And we still have the pipe that blows bubbles of light. If it works as we were told, it may be of use."

They bundled up their wet clothes, collected their few remaining possessions from the ground, and began to walk towards the city.

110

Lief's eyes prickled with weariness, and his feet dragged in the high red boots. The thought of the rat horde, crawling and fighting inside the crumbling towers ahead, filled him with dread. How could they enter the city without being covered and torn to pieces?

Yet enter it they must. For already the Belt of Deltora had begun to grow warm around Lief's waist. One of the lost gems was indeed hidden in the city. The Belt could feel it.

15 - The City

The towers of the city rose dark and forbidding above their heads. Long ago, the great iron entrance gates had fallen and rusted away. Now all that remained was a gaping hole in the wall. The hole led into darkness, and from the darkness drifted a terrible, stealthy, scrabbling sound and the stink of rats. There was something else, too. Something worse. A sense of ancient evil — spiteful, cold, terrifying.

Lief, Barda, and Jasmine began drawing on the Ra-Kachar gloves and covering their faces and heads with the red fabric they had worn during the escape from Noradz.

"I do not understand how the rats became so many," Lief said. "Rats breed quickly, it is true. And they breed faster when there is dark, and dirt, and food is left where they can find it. But why did the people of this city not see the problem, and put a stop to it before it became so great that they had to flee?"

"Some evil was at work." Barda stared grimly at the crumbling walls before them. "The Shadow Lord — "

"You cannot blame the Shadow Lord for everything!" Jasmine burst out suddenly.

Barda and Lief glanced at her in surprise. Her brows were knitted in a frown.

"I have kept silent for too long," she muttered. "But now I will speak, though you will not like what I say. That stranger we saw in Tom's shop — the man with the scar on his face — spoke of the thorns on the plain. He called them the Del King's thorns. And he was right!"

They were staring. She took a deep breath, and hurried on.

"The Shadow Lord has ruled Deltora for only sixteen years. But it has taken far longer than that for the thorns to cover the plain. The sorceress Thaegan's enchantment at the Lake of Tears began a *hundred* years ago. The people of Noradz have been living as they do for centuries. And this evil place must have been abandoned by its people for just as long."

She fell silent, staring moodily ahead.

"What are you saying, Jasmine?" asked Barda impatiently.

The girl's eyes darkened. "The kings and queens

of Deltora betrayed their trust. They shut themselves up in the palace at Del, living in luxury while the land went to ruin and evil prospered."

"That is true," said Lief. "But — "

"I know what you are going to say!" Jasmine snapped. "You have told me before that they were deceived by servants of the Shadow Lord. That they followed stupid rules blindly, thinking that this alone was their duty. But I do not believe that *anyone* could be so blind. I think the whole story is a lie."

Barda and Lief were silent. Both could see why Jasmine would find the truth so hard to believe. She had fended for herself since she was five years old. She was strong and independent. She would never have allowed herself to be a puppet, dancing as a Chief Advisor pulled the strings.

Now she was rushing on. "We are risking our lives to restore the Belt of Deltora. And why? To return power to the royal heir — who even now is hiding, while Deltora suffers and we face danger. But do we really *want* kings and queens back in the palace at Del, lying to us and using us as they did before? I do not think so!"

She glared at them both, and waited.

Barda was angry. To him, what Jasmine was saying was treason. But Lief felt differently.

"I used to think as you do, Jasmine," he said. "I hated the memory of the old King. But questions about whether he and his son were vain and idle or simply foolish, and whether their heir is worthy, are not important now."

"Not *important*?" Jasmine cried. "How can you — ?"

"Jasmine, nothing is more important than ridding our land of the Shadow Lord!" Lief broke in. "However bad things were in Deltora before, at least then the people were free, and not in constant fear."

"Of course!" she exclaimed. "But — "

"We cannot defeat the Shadow Lord by arms. His sorcery is too powerful. Our only hope is the Belt, worn by Adin's true heir. So we are not risking our lives for the royal family, but for our land and all its people! Do you not see that?"

His words struck home. Jasmine paused and blinked. Slowly, the fire in her eyes died. "You are right," she said flatly, at last. "My anger made me lose sight of our main purpose. I am sorry."

She said nothing more, but finished winding the red cloth around her head and face. Then, dagger in hand, she went with them, into the city.

✳

They plunged into a maze of darkness, and the walls were alive with sound. The rats came in the thousands, streaming from cracks in the crumbling stone, their tails lashing like whips, their red eyes gleaming.

Lief took the pipe and blew. Glowing bubbles rose from it, warming and brightening, lighting the darkness like tiny, floating lanterns.

The great rush of rats slowed, became a confused rabble, as most of the creatures scrabbled away from the light, shrieking in panic.

The bravest, darting in the shadows of the ground, tried to cling to the strangers' moving feet, to climb their legs. But the high, slippery boots and smooth, thick red garments defeated all but a few, and these Lief, Barda, and Jasmine could brush off with their gloved hands.

"These garments might have been made for our purpose," muttered Barda, as they struggled along. "It is a fortunate chance that we came by them."

"And a fortunate chance that Tom gave us this pipe," answered Lief. But even as he spoke he wondered. *Were* these things just chance? Or were they — something else? Had he not felt before, on this great journey, that somehow their steps were being guided by an unseen hand?

Brushing, shuddering, they stumbled forward. Now and again Lief blew on the pipe and new bubbles of soft light bloomed. The bubbles they had left behind drifted high above their heads, glowing on the ancient timbers that still supported the roof. The rats had not been able to gnaw through these timbers — or perhaps they knew better than to try, for without them the roof would cave in, exposing the city to the sun.

The whole city was like one huge building — a maze of stone that seemed to have no ending. There was no fresh air, no natural light. This, it seemed, was the way towns were built in these parts, Lief thought. Noradz had been the same.

Everywhere were the signs of vanished grandeur. Carvings, high arches, vast rooms, huge fireplaces filled with ashes, great, echoing kitchens heaped with dust.

And everywhere, rats crawled.

Lief's foot kicked against something that clanged and rolled. The rats caught at his gloves as he bent to pick it up.

It was a carved goblet — silver, he thought, though stained and tarnished with age and neglect. His heart was heavy as he turned it in his hands. It was as though it spoke to him of the people who had fled their home so long ago. He peered at it more closely. Somehow it seemed familiar. But why . . . ?

"Lief!" growled Barda, his voice muffled by the cloth around his mouth and nose. "Keep moving, I beg you. We do not know how long the light pipe will last, and by nightfall we must be in a place of safety."

"Somewhere, at least, where there are no rats," added Jasmine. Furiously, she swept her hands from her shoulders to her hips, so that the rats crawling on her body fell squeaking to the ground.

A vivid memory, and a rush of astonished understanding, jolted Lief to his core. "And if we find such a place, we will say, 'No rats here,' and it will be a blessing," he murmured.

"What?" Jasmine demanded crossly.

There was no time to explain now. Lief made himself move on, pushing the stem of the goblet into his Belt. Later, he would tell Jasmine and Barda. When they were out of danger. When . . .

Come to me, Lief of Del.

Lief started, looking around wildly. What was that? Who had spoken?

"Lief, what is the matter?" Jasmine's voice seemed distant, though she was right beside him. He looked down at her puzzled green eyes. Dimly he realized that she could hear nothing.

Come to me. I am waiting.

The voice hissed and coiled in Lief's mind. Hardly knowing what he was doing, he began to move fast and blindly, following its call.

The bubbles of light floated before him, shining on ruined walls, rusted metal brackets where torches had once burned, fragments of pots piled in heaps. Rats teemed in corners and clawed at his boots.

He stumbled towards the city's heart. The air grew thick and hard to breathe. The Belt around his waist throbbed with heat.

"Lief!" he heard Barda shout. But he could not turn, or answer. He had reached a wide passage. At the end loomed a vast doorway. A sickening, musky smell billowed from whatever was beyond. He faltered, but still he moved on.

He reached the doorway. Inside, something huge moved in darkness.

"Who are you?" he quavered.

And the hissing voice struck at him, piercing and burning.

I am the One. I am Reeah. Come to me.

16 ~ Reeah

Darkness. Evil. Fear.

Trembling, Lief put the pipe to his mouth, and blew. Glowing bubbles drifted upward, lighting what had once been a vast meeting hall.

A giant snake rose, hissing, in the center of the echoing space. The coils of its shining body, as thick as the trunk of an ancient tree, filled the floor from edge to edge. Its eyes were flat, cold, and filled with ancient wickedness. On its head was a crown. And in the center of the crown was a gem that flashed with all the colors of the rainbow.

The opal.

Lief took a step forward.

Stop!

Lief did not know if the word was in his mind, or if the snake had hissed it aloud. He stood motionless. Barda and Jasmine came up behind him. He heard them draw breath sharply, and felt their arms move as they raised their weapons.

Remove the thing you wear under your clothes. Cast it away.

Lief's fingers slowly moved to the Belt around his waist.

"No, Lief!" he heard Barda whisper urgently.

But still he fumbled with the Belt's fastening, trying to loosen it. Nothing seemed real — nothing but the voice that was commanding him.

"Lief!" Jasmine's hard brown hand gripped his wrist, tugging at it furiously.

Lief struggled to shake her off. And then, all at once, it was as if he had woken from a dream. He looked down, blinking.

The palm of his hand was resting on the golden topaz. So it was this that had cleared his mind, and broken the great snake's power over him. Beside the topaz the ruby glimmered. It was no longer bloodred, but pink, showing danger. Yet still it seemed to glow with strange power.

The giant snake hissed in fury and bared its terrible fangs. Its forked tongue flicked in and out. Lief felt the tug of its will, but pressed his hand onto the topaz even harder, and resisted it.

"Why does it not attack?" breathed Jasmine.

But by now, Lief knew. He had remembered some lines from *The Belt of Deltora* — lines about the powers of the ruby.

✝ **The great ruby, symbol of happiness, red as blood, grows pale in the presence of evil, or when misfortune threatens its wearer. It wards off evil spirits, and is an antidote to snake venom.**

"It feels the power of the ruby," he whispered back. "This is why it is fixing its attention on me."

Your magic is strong, Lief of Del, but not strong enough to save you, hissed the snake.

Lief staggered as again its will struck at his mind.

"The opal is in its crown," he panted to Jasmine and Barda. "Do what you can while I distract it!"

Ignoring their whispered warnings, he began edging away from them. The snake turned its head to follow him with hard, cold eyes.

"How do you know my name?" Lief demanded, holding the topaz tightly.

I have the gem that shows the future. I am all-powerful. I am Reeah, the Master's chosen one.

"And who is your master?"

The one who gave my kingdom to me. The one they call the Shadow Lord.

Lief heard Jasmine make a stifled sound, but did not turn to look at her. Instead, he held Reeah's gaze, trying to keep his mind blank.

"Surely you have been here for a very long time, Reeah," he called. "You are so large, so magnificent!"

The snake hissed, raising its head proudly. As Lief had thought, its vanity was as great as its size.

A tender worm I was when first I came into the cellars beneath this city. A race of snivelling humans lived here, then. In their ignorance and fear they would have killed me, had they found me. But the Master had servants among them, and these were awaiting me. They welcomed me, and brought me rats to feed upon, till I grew strong.

Out of the corner of his eye Lief caught a glimpse of Jasmine. She was climbing one of the columns that supported the roof. Gritting his teeth, he forced his mind away from her. It was vital that Reeah's attention remain with him.

"What servants?" he called. "Who were they?"

You know them, hissed Reeah. *They are branded with his mark. They have been promised eternal life and power in his service. You wear their garments, to deceive me. But I am not deceived.*

"Of course you are not!" Lief cried. "I was testing you, to see if you could really see into my mind. Who else would have known where to find rats, what would make them breed, and how to trap them? Who else but the city's rat catchers? It was a clever plan."

Ah, yes, hissed Reeah. *There were few rats, then. My kingdom had not yet achieved the glory of its destiny. But my Master had chosen his servants well. They bred more rats for me — more rats, and more. Until at last the walls teemed with them, and disease spread, and all the food of the city was consumed. And then the people begged the rat catchers to save them, little knowing that they were the very ones who had caused the plague.*

Its wicked eyes glowed with triumph.

"So the rat catchers seized power," said Lief. "They said that the rat plague had come through the people's own wickedness, and that there was nothing left but to flee."

Yes. Across the river to another place where they would build again. When they were gone, I came up from beneath, and claimed my kingdom.

Lief felt, rather than saw, that Jasmine was beginning to walk along the great beam that spanned the hall right beside the great snake's head — walking as easily and lightly as she had walked along branches in the Forests of Silence. But what was her plan? Surely she did not think her daggers could pierce those shining scales? And where was Barda?

The great snake was growing restless. Lief could feel it. Its tongue was flicking in and out. Its head was bending towards him.

"Reeah! The new city is called No Rats — Noradz," he shouted. "I have seen it. The people have forgotten what they once were, and where they came from. Their fear of rats has broken their spirit. The rat catchers are called Ra-Kacharz now, and are like priests, keeping sacred laws. They carry whips like the tails of rats. They are all-powerful. The people live in fear and slavery, serving your Master's purpose."

It is good, hissed Reeah. *It is what they deserve. So*

you have told your story, Lief of Del. Your pitiful magic, your puny weapons, and your smooth tongue have amused me — for a time. But now I am sick of your chatter.

Without warning, it struck. Lief slashed with his sword to protect himself, but the snake's first sweep struck the weapon from his hand as if it were a toy. It spun away from him, circling high into the air.

"Jasmine!" Lief cried. But there was no time to see if Jasmine had caught the sword. The snake was about to strike again. Its huge jaws were open, its fangs dripping with poison.

"Lief! The fire beads!" Barda's voice sounded from the other end of the hall. He must have crept there, to try to attack the monster from behind. The giant snake's tail lashed, and to his horror, Lief saw Barda's body crash into a column and lie still.

The fire beads. Desperately, Lief felt in his pockets, found the jar, and threw it, hard, straight at his enemy's open mouth. But Reeah was too fast for him. The wicked head jerked to one side. The jar sailed past it, smashing uselessly into a column and bursting in a ball of flames.

And then it was only Lief and Reeah.

You are mine, Lief of Del!

The huge head lunged forward with terrifying speed. And the next moment the great snake was raising itself, triumphant, Lief's body dangling from its jaws.

Up, up to the rafters, the hot breath burning . . .

I will swallow you whole. And your magic with you.

There was smoke. There was a crackling sound. Dimly Lief realized that the flames had raced up the column and were licking at the old wood of the rafters.

The fire will not save you. When I have devoured you I will put it out with one gust of my breath. For I am Reeah, the all-powerful. I am Reeah, the One . . .

Through a dizzy haze of terror and pain, through a film of smoke that stung his eyes, Lief saw Jasmine, balancing on a beam beside him. His sword was swinging in her hand. She had torn the red covering from her face. Her teeth were bared in savage fury. She raised her arm . . .

And with a mighty slash she swung the sword, slitting the monster's throat from edge to edge.

Lief heard a hoarse, bubbling cry. He felt the beast's jaws open. He was falling, hurtling towards the ground, the hard stones rushing up to meet him.

And then — there was nothing.

17 - Hope

Groaning, Lief stirred. There was a sweet taste on his lips, and he could hear a crackling sound, a tearing, chewing sound, and shouting, very far away.

He opened his eyes. Jasmine and Barda were leaning over him, calling his name. Jasmine was screwing the top back onto a small jar attached to a chain around her neck. Dimly, Lief realized that he had been given nectar from the Lilies of Life. It had saved him — perhaps brought him back to life as once it had done for Barda.

"I — I am well," he mumbled, struggling to sit up. He looked around. The hall was filled with flickering shadows. Flames, begun and spread by the blazing fire beads, roared in the ancient rafters. The giant snake lay dead on the floor, its body covered by gnawing rats. More rats were streaming from the walls and through the doorway, fighting one another to reach the feast.

For hundreds of years it has eaten them, thought Lief, dazed. Now they are eating it. Even fear of fire will not stop them.

"We must get out! Out!" Barda was shouting.

Lief felt himself pulled to his feet and slung over Barda's shoulder. His head was spinning. He wanted to cry out, "What of the crown? The opal?"

But then he saw that the crown was in Barda's hand.

Limp as a doll, he was carried through burning hallways. Jolting on Barda's back, he closed his stinging eyes against the smoke.

When he looked again, they were staggering through the city gateway onto the dark plain and Kree, squawking anxiously, was soaring to meet them. There was a tremendous crash from behind them. The roof of the city had begun to fall.

On they went, and on, till they had nearly reached the river.

"I can walk," Lief managed to croak. Barda stopped and put him gently on the ground. His legs trembled, but he stood upright, turning to look at the burning city.

"I never thought I'd see you stand on your own two feet again, my friend," Barda said cheerfully. "That fall Jasmine gave you was — "

"It was let him fall or see him disappear into the

128

snake's belly," exclaimed Jasmine. "Which do you think was better?"

She handed Lief's sword to him. It gleamed in the moonlight, its blade still dark with Reeah's blood.

"Jasmine — " Lief began. But she shrugged and turned away, pretending to be busy coaxing Filli out onto her shoulder. He saw that she was embarrassed at the idea that he would try to thank her for saving his life.

"Do you think it is safe to rest here?" he asked instead. "Having recently had every bone in my body broken, I do not think I could face crossing the river yet."

Barda nodded. "Quite safe, I think. For a while, at least, there will be no rats here." Then his teeth gleamed as he grinned and brushed his hands from shoulder to hip. "Noradzeer," he added.

"Lief, how did you know, before the snake told you, that the people of Noradz had once lived in the City of the Rats?" Jasmine demanded.

"There were many clues," Lief said tiredly. "But, perhaps, I would not have seen the connection if I had not found this." He pulled the tarnished goblet from his Belt and held it out to them.

"Why, it is a pair to the goblet that held the Life and Death cards — the sacred Cup of Noradz," said Barda, taking it in his hands and looking at it with wonder. "It must have been dropped and left behind when the people fled the city."

Lief smiled as Filli's small black nose peeped over Jasmine's collar to see what was happening.

"No wonder Filli frightened the people in Noradz," he said.

"He looks nothing like a rat!" Jasmine exclaimed indignantly.

"They hate anything small with fur. It must be a fear taught to them from their earliest days," said Barda.

Lief nodded. "Like the fear of dropping food on the ground, or leaving dishes uncovered, because such things once attracted rats in the hundreds. Or the fear of eating food that has been spoiled, as it often was in the days of the plague. The need for such great care passed hundreds of years ago. But the Ra-Kacharz have seen to it that the fear remains, and keeps the people in bondage to them — and to the Shadow Lord."

Lief was speaking lightly and idly, to blot from his mind the horrible things that had just happened to him. But Jasmine looked at him seriously, her head to one side.

"Plainly, then, it is quite possible for a people to forget their history, and to follow foolish rules out of duty, if they are born to it," she said. "I would not have believed it. But now I have seen it with my own eyes."

Lief realized that this was her way of saying that she was beginning to think that the kings and queens of Deltora had been less to blame than she had thought. Of this, he was very glad.

"Mind you," Jasmine added quickly, as he smiled, "there is always a choice, and bonds can be broken. The girl Tira helped us, though she feared." She paused. "One day, I hope, we can go back for her and set her free. Make them all free, if they wish it."

"This is our best chance of doing so." Lief unfastened the Belt and laid it before him on the hard ground of the plain. Then Barda handed him the crown that held the great opal.

As it neared the Belt, the opal fell from the crown into Lief's hand. His mind was suddenly filled with a vision of sandy wastes, of lowering, clouded skies. He saw himself, alone, among rippling dunes that had no ending. And he felt terror lurking, unseen. He gasped in horror.

He looked up and saw Jasmine and Barda watching him anxiously. He closed his trembling hand more tightly around the gem.

"I had forgotten," he said huskily, trying to smile. "The opal gives glimpses of the future. It seems that this may not always be a blessing."

Fearing that they might ask him what he had seen, he bent to fit the stone into the Belt. Under his fingers, its rainbow colors seemed to flash and burn like fire. Abruptly, his racing heart quietened, the fear faded, and a tingling warmth took its place.

"The opal is also the symbol of hope," Barda murmured, watching him.

Lief nodded, pressing his hand over the dancing colors, feeling the gem's power flood through him. And when finally he looked up, his face was at peace.

"So now we have the topaz for faith, the ruby for happiness, and the opal for hope," he said quietly. "What will be next?"

Jasmine held up her arm to Kree, who fluttered down to her with a glad screech. "Whatever the fourth stone is, surely it will not lead us into worse danger than the other three."

"And if it does?" Barda teased.

She shrugged. "We will face what comes," she said simply.

Lief lifted the Belt from the ground and fastened it around his waist. It warmed against his skin — solid, safe, and a little heavier than before. Faith, happiness, hope, he thought, and his heart swelled with all three.

"Yes," he said. "We will face what comes. Together."

The Deltora Book of Monsters

by Josef

Palace Librarian in the reign of King Alton

This book has been compiled in secret. If the work had been discovered by any authority, I, its author, would have paid with my life. Or so I believe.

The risk was worth taking. Forces are working in Deltora to suppress the facts of our past as well as those of our present. Lies are everywhere. King Alton believes that the kingdom is thriving. He thinks that if monstrous perils once existed in far-flung corners, they exist no longer.

I know this is false. Because I, who once wore the silken gloves and velvet tunic of a palace librarian, now scavenge for food in the gutters of Del. I now know what the common people know, and more. I could never have imagined such a future for myself. But I regret nothing.

Perhaps I would never have fled from the palace if the king's chief advisor, Prandine, had not ordered me to burn *The Deltora Annals*. The threatened destruction of the *Annals*, that great, vivid picture of Deltora over the ages, was more than I could bear. And so it was that while pretending to obey Prandine's order, I saved the *Annals* and myself.

This book contains material drawn from *The Deltora Annals* as well as new information I have gained in the past few years. It describes many of the dreadful, mysterious beings that haunt this land. Some of these creatures are as evil and unnatural as their master in the Shadowlands. Others are native to Deltora. All grow stronger every day. Yet the king does nothing to offer his people protection. They hate him for it. But why should he help, since he does not know the monsters exist?

None of them are spoken of in the palace except as beasts of legend, dangers of the past.

Books such as this are needed to correct the lies that have become official truth. The people are too busy scraping a living to write down what they know. Writing, in fact, seems almost to have disappeared among them. I fear that lies may one day become the only "facts" available to students, unless people like me act to prevent it.

What the future holds for us, and for Deltora, I cannot say. But when my hopes dim, I take heart in remembering another thing I did before I left the palace. It concerns yet another book — *The Belt of Deltora*. It is simply written, but full of wisdom. From the day I first found it in the library, I believed that it was of vital importance, and that it contained the keys to Deltora's future, as well as its past. I kept it hidden, for I knew that if Prandine saw it, it would quietly disappear. I had planned to take it with me, but at the last moment something moved me to change my mind. I hid it, instead, in a dim corner where it would only be discovered by an eager searcher.

I cling to the hope that one day Prince Endon might find it. Even Endon's friend, young Jarred, might do so, for though Jarred has no great love of books, his wits are keen. He may remember the library if one day he is in urgent need of knowledge. I know in my heart that if Deltora has a future, it lies with these young ones. It would be my joy to know that in some small way I have helped their cause. In faith —

Josef
Writing in the city of Del in the 35th year of the reign of King Alton.

Thaegan's Children

The names of Thaegan's evil brood are: Hot, Tot, Pik, Snik, Jin, Jod, Fie, Fly, Zan, Zod, Lun, Lod, and Ichabod.

I gained knowledge of their names and appearance from an unfortunate man I found cringing by the city gates. He was ragged and starving. His mind had been clouded by horror. He was the only one of five travellers to have escaped the clutches of Thaegan's children. His companions were roasted alive and eaten. He was to be the last in the fire, but before his time came the monsters, bloated, fell asleep. He managed to escape to stumble back to Del.

He could not even remember his own name, but the picture of Thaegan's children as he had seen them was burned into his brain. From his

hideous descriptions this picture was painted.

Jin is green-white, and grossly fat. She has yellow tusks, and three stubby horns sprout from the back of her skull. Jod has metal spikes for teeth, and there are just two flaring nostrils where his nose should be. Fie and Fly are green with large heads and dripping brown fangs. Hot and Tot are small and yellow. Zan has six stumpy legs. Pik and Snik are covered in brown hair. Lan and Lod are pale and bald. Zod is covered in lumps. Ichabod is huge, and slimy red. I have not labelled the monsters. But you, dear reader, can I am sure pick out which one is which. Unless you wish simply to turn your gaze away, and flick over the page. I would not blame you.

Muddlets

Perhaps some will consider that I am wrong to include Muddlets in this book. Muddlets are not "monsters" in the sense of being savage or wicked. They do not have teeth, claws, spines, or poison. They eat only grass, moss, apples, and certain leaves. And they are by all reports very good-natured.

Nevertheless, they are such strange, self-willed creatures that I decided they deserved a place in this collection. They have carried many unknowing riders into danger.

Wild herds of Muddlets once roamed the Plains country, especially in the area now known as the Plain of the Rats. According to *The Deltora Annals* they numbered many, many thousands, and to be caught in a Muddlet stampede was a terrifying and life-threatening experience. Over the years, as towns and villages grew and the Plain of the Rats was eaten bare by the multiplying rats, herd numbers grew less. Wild Muddlets are now rarely seen, though they still exist.

Muddlets have extraordinary speed and strength. For thousands of years they have been captured by Plains people for use as beasts of burden. But they do not make reliable domestic animals.

However tame they may seem, they cannot be relied upon to do anything other than what they wish. No matter what their training may have been, for example, they will bolt at the sight of any small, furred animal. They will also ignore all instructions if

they smell their home field or over-ripe apples (their favorite food), even plunging into deep water, over cliffs, and into quicksand to reach their goal.

Despite this, Muddlets are still used by some Plains folk. The Ra-Kacharz of Noradz are among those who still keep a Muddlet herd. But any traveller who may be tempted by the Muddlets' low price should think twice before following their example. Muddlets are not beasts to trust.

Ready to return to the land of
magic and dragons?
Turn the page for a sneak peek of

EMILY RODDA

THE
GOLDEN DOOR

a new tale from the world of
Deltora

THE BROTHERS

It was the season for skimmers, and this year more skimmers than ever were coming over the Wall of Weld.

From dusk till dawn, the beasts flapped down through the cloud that shrouded the top of the Wall. They showered on the dark city like giant, pale falling leaves, leathery wings rasping, white eyes gleaming, needle teeth glinting in the dark.

The skimmers came for food. They came to feast on the warm-blooded creatures, animal and human, that lived within the Wall of Weld.

On the orders of the Warden, the usual safety notices had been put up all over the city. Few people bothered to read them, because they were always the same. But this year, in Southwall, where Lisbeth the beekeeper lived with her three sons, they had been covered with disrespectful scrawls.

ATTENTION, CITIZENS OF WELD!
SKIMMER SAFETY

- Stay in your homes between dusk and dawn. *so the Skimmers know where to find you*
- Seal your windows, doors and chimneys. *because Skimmers like a challenge!*
- Note that skimmers are almost blind, but are attracted by signs of life such as movement, light, heat, smell and sound. *so stop breathing!*

- As is my duty, I cast the traditional spells of protection over Weld each day but please remember—your safety by night is your responsibility! *though I know I have less magic in me than a Weld goat* *Not mine - I am tucked up safe in the Keep, HA, HA!*

USELESS
The Warden of Weld

No one knew who was writing on the notices — or so the people of Southwall claimed when the Keep soldiers questioned them. Like everyone else in Weld, the Southwall citizens were very law-abiding. Most would never have dreamed of damaging one of the Warden's notices themselves. But many secretly agreed with the person who had done so.

Rye, the youngest of Lisbeth's sons, had the half-thrilled, half-fearful suspicion that his eldest brother, Dirk, might be responsible.

Dirk worked on the Wall as his father had done, repairing and thickening Weld's ancient defense against the barbarians on the coast of the island of Dorne. Brave, strong, and usually good-natured, Dirk had become increasingly angry about the Warden's failure to protect Weld from the skimmer attacks.

Sholto, the middle brother, thin, cautious, and clever, said little, but Rye knew he agreed with Dirk. Sholto worked for Tallus, the Southwall healer, learning how to mend broken bones and mix potions. The soldiers had questioned him when they had come to the healer's house seeking information. Rye had overheard him telling Dirk about it.

"Do not worry," Sholto had drawled when Dirk asked him anxiously what he had said in answer to the questions. "If I cannot bamboozle those fancily dressed oafs, I am not the man you think I am."

And Dirk had clapped him on the shoulder and shouted with laughter.

Rye hoped fervently that the soldiers would not question him, and to his relief, so far they had not. Rye was still at school, and no doubt the soldiers thought he was too young to know anything of importance.

As the clouded sky dimmed above them, and the Wall darkened around their city, the people of Weld closed their shutters and barred their doors.

Those who still followed the old magic ways sprinkled salt on their doorsteps and window ledges and chanted the protective spells of their ancestors. Those who no longer believed in such things merely stuffed rags and straw into the chinks in their mud-brick walls, and hoped for the best.

Lisbeth's family did all these things, and more.

Lisbeth sprinkled the salt and murmured the magic words. Dirk, tall and fair, followed her around the house, fastening all the locks. Dark, lean Sholto trailed them like a shadow, pressing rags soaked in the skimmer repellent he had invented into the gaps between the shutters and the crack beneath the door.

And Rye, red-haired and eager, watched them all as he did his own humble duty, clearing the table of Sholto's books and setting out the cold, plain food that was always eaten at night in skimmer season.

Later, in dimness, the three brothers and their mother huddled around the table, talking in whispers, listening to the hateful, dry rustling of the skimmers' wings outside.

"Folk at the market were saying that there was a riot in Northwall this morning," Lisbeth murmured. "They said that the Warden's signs were set on fire, and the crowd fought with the soldiers who tried to stop the damage. Can this be true? Citizens of *Weld* acting like barbarians?"

"It is true enough," Sholto said, pressing a hard-boiled duck egg against his plate to crack the pale blue shell as noiselessly as he could. "Skimmers killed three families in Northwall last night. It is only the first riot of many, I fear. When people are afraid, they do not think before they act."

Dirk snorted. "They are sick of the Warden's excuses. And they are right. Everyone on the Wall was talking of it today."

"And you most of all, Dirk, I imagine," said Sholto drily.

Dirk's eyes flashed. "Why not? It is obvious to everyone that a new leader must have risen among the barbarians — a warlord determined to conquer Weld at last. Every year, more skimmers come. Every year, we lose more food and more lives, and work on the Wall falls further behind. The Enemy is weakening us, little by little."

"We do not know there *is* an Enemy, Dirk," Sholto muttered. "For all we know, the skimmers come here of their own accord. For skimmers, Weld may be nothing but a giant feeding bowl, in which tender prey are conveniently trapped."

Rye's stomach turned over.

"Sholto!" Lisbeth scolded. "Do not say such things! Especially in front of Rye!"

"Why not in front of me?" Rye demanded stoutly, though the bread in his mouth seemed to have turned to dust. "I am not a baby!"

Sholto shrugged, carefully picking the last scrap of shell from his egg.

"We might as well face the truth," he said calmly. "A wall that cannot be climbed, and which has no gates, is all very well when it keeps dangers out. But it works two ways. It also makes prisoners of those who are inside it."

He bit into the egg and chewed somberly.

"The skimmers are being deliberately bred and sent!" Dirk insisted. "If they were natural to Dorne, they would have been flying over the Wall from the beginning. But the attacks began only five years ago!"

Sholto merely raised one eyebrow and took another bite.

Dirk shook his head in frustration. "Ah, what does it matter anyway?" he said, pushing his plate away as if he had suddenly lost his appetite. "What does it matter *why* the skimmers invade? They *do* invade — that is the important thing! Weld is under attack. And the Warden does nothing!"

"His soldiers fill the skimmer poison traps," Lisbeth murmured, anxious to restore peace at the table. "He has said that orphaned children can be cared for at the Keep. And he has at last agreed that the end-of-work bell should be rung an hour earlier, so people can arrive home well before —"

"At last!" Dirk broke in impatiently. "That is the point, Mother! The Warden has taken *years* to do things that a good leader would have done at once! If the Warden had not delayed cutting the hours of work, Father would not have been on the Wall at sunset in the third skimmer season. He would still be with us now!"

"Don't, Dirk!" whispered Rye, seeing his mother bowing her head and biting her lip.

"I have to speak of it, Rye," said Dirk, his voice rising. "Our father was just one of hundreds of Wall workers who fell prey to skimmers because of the Warden's dithering!"

"Hush!" Sholto warned, raising his eyes to the ceiling to remind his brother of the skimmers flying above. And Dirk fell silent, pressing his lips together and clenching his fists.

✳

Like all the other citizens of Weld in skimmer season, Lisbeth and her sons went to bed early. What else was there to do, when sound was dangerous and the smallest chink of light might lead to a skimmer attack?

Rye lay in the room he shared with his brothers, listening to the rush of wings outside the shutters, the occasional scrabbling of claws on the roof.

He prayed that the wings would pass them by. He prayed that he, his mother, and his brothers would not wake, like those ill-fated families in Northwall, to find skimmers filling the house, and death only moments away.

He crossed his fingers, then crossed his wrists, in the age-old Weld gesture that was supposed to ward off evil. He closed his eyes and tried to relax, but he knew that sleep would not come easily. The closely shuttered room was stuffy and far too warm. Sholto's words at the dinner table kept echoing in his mind.

Weld may be nothing but a giant feeding bowl, in which tender prey are conveniently trapped. . . .

From Rye's earliest years, he had been told that inside the Wall of Weld there was safety, as long as the laws laid down by the Warden were obeyed.

Certainly, the laws were many. Sometimes even Rye had complained that they were *too* many.

He had nodded vigorously when Sholto had sneered that the citizens of Weld were treated like children too young to decide for themselves what was dangerous and what was not.

He had laughed when Dirk had made fun of the Warden's latest notices: *Citizens of Weld! Dress warmly in winter to avoid colds and chills. Children of Weld! Play wisely! Rough games lead to broken bones. . . .*

But at least he had felt safe — safe within the Wall.

Lying very still, his wrists crossed rigidly on his chest, Rye thought about that. He thought about Weld, and its Wall. Thought about the history he had learned and taken for granted. Thought, for the first time, about what that history meant.

Weld had existed for almost a thousand years, ever since its founder, the great sorcerer Dann, had fled with his followers from the savage barbarians and monstrous creatures that infested the coast of Dorne.

Turning his back on the sea, Dann had taken his people to a place where the barbarians dared not follow. He had led them through the dangerous, forbidden ring of land called the Fell Zone, to the secret center of the island. And there, within a towering Wall, he had created a place of peace, safety, and magic — the city of Weld.

After Dann's time, the magic had slowly faded, but his Wall had remained. More than half of the city's workers labored on it every day, repairing and strengthening it. Every rock and stone in Weld, except for the stones that formed the Warden's Keep, had vanished into the Wall's vast bulk centuries ago. The workers used bricks of mud and straw to mend and thicken it now.

And as the Wall had thickened, little by little, it had crept ever closer to the great trench at its base — the trench from which the clay for bricks was dug.

The trench now circled Weld in the Wall's shadow like a deep, ugly scar. In the past, houses had been pulled down to make way for it. Soon, everyone knew, more would have to go.

The people did not complain. They knew that the Wall, and the Fell Zone beyond it, kept Weld safe. They had thought it always would.

Then the first skimmers had come. And now, after five years of invasions, it was clear to everyone that the days of safety were over.

The barbarians had at last found a way to attack Weld. Not by tunneling through the base of the Wall, as had always been feared, but by breeding creatures that could do what had once seemed impossible — brave the Wall's great height and fly over it.

And we are trapped inside, Rye thought.

Tender prey . . .

"This room is stifling!" he heard Dirk mutter to Sholto in the darkness. "I cannot breathe! Sholto, this cannot go on! The Warden must act!"

"Perhaps he will," Sholto whispered back. "The riot in Northwall must have shaken him. Tomorrow may bring some surprises."

Emily Rodda is the author of the *New York Times* bestselling Deltora Quest series, with over two million copies of her books in print. Winner of the Children's Book Council of Australia's Book of the Year Award [Younger Readers] a record five times, Emily lives in Sydney, Australia.